"He c...

man, this Englishman."

Jourdain continued harshly. "You still have your virginity."

"Some men," Brooke flung back, "have more respect than to want a girl to—" she faltered "—to go against her values and give herself to s-satisfy a man's momentary lust."

"*Mon Dieu,*" he exclaimed, astonished at such a viewpoint. "What sort of a man have you that he cannot stir the passion I have seen in you?"

"Oh, for goodness' sake!" Brooke erupted. "He's a man who certainly wouldn't creep up on a girl and kiss her while she was asleep."

Jourdain looked at her for long seconds. "Would you say you are fully awake now?"

Warily she nodded, then realized she should have shaken her head. But even as she made a move away, his head came down and his mouth claimed hers in a kiss....

Jessica Steele first tried her hand at writing romance novels at her husband's encouragement two years after they were married. She fondly remembers the day her first novel was accepted for publication. "Peter mopped me up, and neither of us cooked that night," she recalls. "We went out to dinner." She and her husband live in a hundred-year-old cottage in Worcestershire, and they've traveled to many fascinating places—such as China, Japan, Mexico and Denmark—that make wonderful settings for her books.

Books by Jessica Steele

HARLEQUIN ROMANCE
2494—BUT KNOW NOT WHY
2502—DISHONEST WOMAN
2555—DISTRUST HER SHADOW
2580—TETHERED LIBERTY
2607—TOMORROW—COME SOON
2687—NO HONOURABLE COMPROMISE
2789—MISLEADING ENCOUNTER
2800—SO NEAR, SO FAR

HARLEQUIN PRESENTS
717—RUTHLESS IN ALL
725—GALLANT ANTAGONIST
749—BOND OF VENGEANCE
766—NO HOLDS BARRED
767—FACADE
836—A PROMISE TO DISHONOUR

Beyond
Her Control

Jessica Steele

Harlequin Books

TORONTO • NEW YORK • LONDON
AMSTERDAM • PARIS • SYDNEY • HAMBURG
STOCKHOLM • ATHENS • TOKYO • MILAN

Original hardcover edition published in 1986
by Mills & Boon Limited

ISBN 0-373-02850-4

Harlequin Romance first edition July 1987

CHAPTER ONE

BEHIND with her chores, Brooke surveyed the greatly reduced laundry load that Tuesday, and was grateful for small mercies. Without doubt the washing machine would be on non-stop when the twins came home; it was a fair bet that Steven would not have rinsed through so much as a handkerchief during his extended camping holiday. Since Stephanie, though, was spending her summer vacation with a French family, Brooke hoped that the younger twin would be more fastidious.

With both her brother and sister away, and with only herself and her father to look after, Brooke still found plenty to do. Apart from the general running of the household, the twins were starting at university in October, and getting them ready was a full-time job.

In the clothes department Steven was not much of a problem. Left to himself, he would wear the same tee-shirt and jeans week in week out—had she allowed it. But Stephanie was another matter; her theme song, 'I've got nothing to wear', had been constant since the day she had discovered that clothes were not just something you left lying around in a crumpled heap.

A contented smile curved Brooke's gently generous mouth. Stephanie would squeal with pleasure when she saw the new additions to her already bulging wardrobe; the sewing machine had been in non-stop service since her father had driven her to catch the cross-Channel ferry.

Brooke's smile dipped at the memory of Stephanie's dramatics when their father had put his foot down about her going to France. A furious argument had developed when Alec Farringdon, of the view that October was soon enough for the baby of the family to leave the nest, had for once become the stern parent.

'You'll have a year in France as part of your language course later on,' he had reminded Stephanie. 'Be content with that.'

Sensing she was losing the argument, Stephanie had promptly changed tack to try to wheedle, coax and cajole. When, to her surprise, her father still remained adamant, she had burst into totally frustrated tears, and with a dramatic, 'I'll just die if you don't let me go!' she had slammed up to her room.

'If only your mother was alive!' Alec Farringdon sighed to his elder daughter. He, Steven and Stephanie were so alike in volatile temperament, with Brooke the only one to take after her even-tempered mother. He asked, as he often did when Stephanie threw a tantrum, 'Go and talk to her, Brooke.'

Brooke owned that between them, though not without reason, they had all taken a hand in spoiling Stephanie. She found her sister sprawled face down on her bed sobbing her heart out, and could not help but feel sorry for her that, when she tried to be so grown up, she always failed miserably when she could not get her own way.

'Come on, chick,' she soothed calmly, 'it can't be as bad as all that.'

'He—doesn't understand,' Stephanie sobbed. 'None of you do!'

'What don't we understand?' Brooke asked gently. She had taken on the woman's role in the home six years ago when their mother had died, but her love for her sister had begun long before then. 'Tell me, darling,' she coaxed, turning her thoughts from all the trauma that had followed her mother's death.

'You just don't—or won't understand how vital it is that I cram in as much French as I can before I go to university,' said Stephanie on a hiccup.

Brooke was well aware of the hard study Stephanie had put in to earn her university place, but it was her opinion that she had crammed enough, and should now be relaxing her brain before the university term began.

However, she said none of what she was thinking. Instead, in the calm way in which she had become accustomed to dealing with each of Stephanie's crises, she asked quietly, 'Can you tell me why it's so vital?'

'You *know* why!'

'So tell me again,' said Brooke patiently, without the first clue to what was going on inside her sister's pretty head.

'Why should I?' Stephanie returned sulkily, her set expression and pouting mouth letting Brooke know that she had donned her awkward-for-the-sake-of-it hat.

'Because if you don't,' Brooke responded evenly, not rising to her belligerent attitude, 'there's no way I shall be able to see your point of view.'

Fifteen minutes later, she had got from Stephanie all that was stewing inside her. All that Stephanie thought they had known without her having to explain because they lived so closely with one another.

Brooke left her and blamed herself, when she knew Stephanie so well, for not seeing how inadequate she felt on account of her frequent bouts of missed schooling.

It was chastening to know, when a natural flair combined with sheer hard slog had won Stephanie a university place to study French, that even that achievement had failed to give her confidence in her ability.

It had made not the smallest difference to Stephanie's anxiety to tell her that all the other students were probably going through the same anxiety she was experiencing. The belief was dyed deeply in Stephanie, that only by spending her summer holiday in France, where she would converse daily in French, would she be able to hold her own when she started her studies in earnest.

Which left Brooke knowing that, somehow, she was going to have to persuade her father to let Stephanie go. Aside from the fact that her young sister would alternately storm and sulk about the place and make life generally unbearable for everyone—and nobody could keep up a sulk like Stephanie could—if going to France would give her the confidence she sought, then it was small compensation for the dreadful time she had been through.

Stephanie had always been mildly asthmatic. At twelve years old, when their much loved and gentle mother had died, Stephanie had almost immediately gone into her first attack of roaring asthma.

It had been a toss-up to know who had been most frightened by that first attack. Stephanie, as she wheezed and laboured for breath, had certainly been terrified. Brooke, four years older than the twins, remembered her own fear that they might lose Stephanie too. While her father, still too deep in shock from losing his wife to be able to cope, had left it to Brooke to watch her sister like a hawk.

Her relief when Stephanie had recovered had been enormous. But another attack had followed, and Brooke had stayed away from school to look after her. She had stayed away from school again when Stephanie had a third attack. But it was when Stephanie came out of that third attack that Brooke had time to observe how, without her mother's calming influence, everything and everyone was going to pieces.

Already, despite her efforts in between cooking, cleaning, attending to her homework and keeping a weather eye on Stephanie, the big rambling home had started to wear a neglected air. She had been hoping to go to university. But to see Steven, who at one time was always up to mischief, and who was never without a grin on his face, now looking so unhappy and so totally bewildered as he mooched aimlessly about, told her that her education could wait.

The loss of their mother would take some getting used to. Brooke's own pain told her she had a long way to go herself. But, with her father so withdrawn into himself that he had to be urged to get up and go to work each morning, Brooke came to a swift and irrevocable decision. She was sixteen, and of a legal age to leave school.

The next morning, without saying a word to her father, she rang her headmaster to tell him she would not be returning to school.

'You can't do that,' he replied kindly, aware from her recent attendance record that she had a home problem.

'I've done it, Mr Varnish,' Brooke told him, politely but firmly.

She had nursed a small suspicion that her father might raise the roof when she told him. But, in his grief, nothing had very much power to affect him.

'Perhaps it's for the best,' was all he said.

Brooke had no cause to regret her decision over the next three years. In that first year, though, a couple of crises saw her pull out all the stops to cope.

Stephanie had her worst attack of asthma ever and was rushed to hospital. When she came home she was in such a state of nerves that she begged Brooke never to let her go into hospital again.

The next thing that happened was that their father lost

the chance to have his own department, when his lack of attention to his research chemist work, saw someone promoted over his head.

'At my age, I'll never get another chance,' he complained, 'Not that I care,' he added, which made Brooke think that care he did. And if he did care about his work again, then maybe he was coming to terms with his grief.

In the year that followed, her father gradually came to be more the man he had been before disaster had struck. Stephanie, though, was still plagued by illness and her absences from school were countless.

Stephanie was still suffering. Steven, however, who without knowing it had also received special attention from his elder sister, was once again more prone to grin his way through his day than to go around with a solemn face.

It was as the twins' fifteenth birthday drew near that the miracle happened: Stephanie said goodbye to asthma!

Unable to believe it, when week after week went by without her sister needing to be dosed with some medication or other, Brooke started to have faith in the docter's pronouncement that some fifty per cent of asthma victims grew out of it as they became older.

When all evidence showed that Stephanie *had* 'grown out of it', and she started to join in with Steven's talk of going to university, an unexpected restlessness entered Brooke's soul. Suddenly, she started to think of her own unfinished education.

When she reached the conclusion that countless other women successfully ran a home *and* held down a full-time job, she went to have a word with her father.

'Do you think it would disrupt things too much if I took a full-time secretarial course, and then got myself a job?' she asked.

'You want to go out to work?' he asked, his incredulous expression revealing that it had never crossed his mind that she might want something more from life than the daily round of looking after them all.

'Nothing will change here,' she assured him quickly, aware that although everyone was feeling far more secure than they had three years previously, they still needed a stable home life. 'Except,' she went on, 'that the twins will have to fend for themselves until I get in in the evenings. But they're both old enough now to make a cup of tea and a sandwich if they can't hang on for dinner.' With her father's blessing, Brooke arranged her secretarial course.

When in the first week of starting her training Stephanie became resentful, and Steven became awkward—deliberately, Brooke felt—she decided it was just a period of adjustment they were going through, and would soon get over. They did not get over it.

A month into her course, Brooke came home to find that Stephanie and Steven had been fighting. Stephanie liked to listen to pop music while she did her homework, Steven did not. Apparently he had gone to her room to tell her to turn the full blast volume down, and one word had led to another until Stephanie had slapped him. Incensed, Steven forgot his caring for her, and had slapped her back. In a fury, Stephanie had charged to his room and had begun throwing his books about, and anything else she could pick up. Steven had retaliated in a similar manner.

For the first time ever, as she saw her secretarial course slipping away, Brooke felt angry enough to bang both their heads together. But Steven was obstinate and refused to apologise, while Stephanie was defiant and damned if she would say sorry. From somewhere Brooke found sufficient control to deal with this crisis as calmly as she handled previous crises.

She had no hope, though, of keeping what had happened from their father. For the twins complained long and bitterly to him about each other during the evening meal. So that by the time the two of them had stomped up the stairs to bed, Alec Farringdon was left in no doubt that all hell had broken loose while he and Brooke were out of the house. So it came as no surprise when Brooke, swallowing her disappointment, told him it did not look as if the time was right for her secretarial course.

'It's not fair that you should give it up, just because those two can't be trusted to behave in a civilised manner,' he complained.

'They're going through a difficult time in their development,' Brooke found herself excusing them.

'*You* never did!' he reminded her. 'You were only a little older than that pair when your mother died and you buckled to, to . . .' His voice faded, his thoughts, Brooke knew, taken up with the wife he had loved so very much.

In the months that followed, Brooke began to see it was meant to be that she should give up her secretarial training. As things turned out, she had not been mistaken when she had said that the twins were going through a difficult time in their development.

Stephanie had always been the more volatile of the two and, whenever life appeared to be going smoothly, she could be relied upon to set the cat amongst the pigeons. But Brooke had learned early on how to cope when her young sister took it into her head to 'liven things up'. Which was why she was a little out of her depth, when Steven became the bigger problem of the two.

Suddenly he was endlessly argumentative and moody, and although Brooke tried hard to understand the antagonistic youngster he had become, it was not easy. With Steven 'anti' just about everything, he was soon at loggerheads with his father.

After one dreadful upset when Steven resented his father's authority, just as he resented anything else he could find to resent, Alec Farringdon came near to boxing his ears.

'You've more patience than me, Brooke,' he told her when the dust had settled, but as if afraid he might yet raise his fist to his son if he had any more of his insolence, he added, 'will you deal with him?'

She could not have said with any conviction that she did a better job than anyone else, but after what seemed like light-years of keeping patience with Steven, suddenly he started to get over his moodiness. One day he came into the kitchen, thrust a bunch of flowers at her and actually kissed her cheek before mumbling something she had not caught, and then promptly disappeared. Brooke felt as though she had received a king's ransom.

The feel of tears from that sweet memory snapped Brooke out of her reverie. Quickly she remembered all she meant to do that day. She did not have time to stand around reviewing the last six years. But she could not resist some small feeling of satisfaction that, despite all the trauma, everything now looked set fair.

Steven would soon be starting his Civil Engineering studies at Aston University, and Stephanie, who with her backing was now in Normandy building up her confidence, would soon be starting her studies at York. Even their father, who had given up all hope of promotion, was to have a second chance. The day after tomorrow, he was to face a promotion panel. As for herself, now that the stabilising influence she had in the home was no longer needed, she was to have a second crack at that secretarial course next month.

A rare feeling of complacency settled over Brooke. She had resumed her chores for only a few minutes, however, when she espied the postman coming up the garden path.

Instantly she went to the hall. A picture postcard had been received from Steven last Friday, so it was unlikely they would hear from him again so soon. Some communication from Stephanie, though, was way over-due. Quite obviously her young sister was enjoying herself, since apart from one letter early on, she had not found another minute in which to put pen to paper.

The envelope the postman pushed through the letter box was addressed to both her and her father, and bore a foreign stamp. Eagerly Brooke picked it up and hurried for the letter-opener.

Withdrawing the contents, she absently noted that her sister was making free use of her host's headed writing paper, and then started to read.

A gasp of pure astonishment was the only sound to be heard in the room as Brooke read on to the end. Then she read through again what Stephanie had so blithely written.

By the time Brooke had, disbelievingly, read the letter a third time, all sign of complacency in her was shattered.

Stunned, she collapsed to the nearest chair, and could not but wonder how she could have allowed herself even a moment's complacency. Hadn't she known from way back that whenever they seemed to be going through a smooth patch, Stephanie could be relied upon to stir things up! Even with Stephanie not at home, not in England, but in another country, she had lost none of her ability to throw a spanner in the works.

Brooke read through Stephanie's letter yet again, and started to get annoyed. Stephanie, it appeared, imagined herself in love with one Monsieur Jourdain Marchais, her host. Brooke re-read through her ravings about how marvellous he was, how sophisticated, how he had been everywhere and had done absolutely everything, and on to Stephanie's, 'I'm quite, quite desperately in love with him', and did not believe it for a moment. Stephanie, who never did things by halves, had already thought herself in love a couple of times before, but her crushes never lasted for more than a few months.

What knocked Brooke for six with this particular crush, though, was Stephanie's fervent avowal, which came at the end. 'My heart,' she declared dramatically, 'is here in France. Which is why I know you will understand and wish me well, when I tell you I've decided not to return to go to university, or even to return to England, but to stay here with my love, Jourdain.'

Wish her well! Brooke felt more like giving her sister a short sharp talking to than wishing her well. It amazed her that when Stephanie had worked so hard to gain her university place, she could talk of giving it up just like that.

A flutter of alarm snatched at Brooke on the realisation that if Stephanie had only just discovered her 'love' for Jourdain Marchais, her university term could be well under way before she decided Monsieur was not so marvellous after all, and came home.

She remembered clearly Stephanie's panic that she would start her course at a disadvantage. It had been the only reason she had been allowed to go to France in the first place. Brooke visualised her being in a worse panic than ever if she had to start her term a month or two after the other students. That was, if the university kept her place open for her!

Stephanie was immature for her years. Brooke knew that without worrying over the fact. It had been her belief that she would mature soon enough when she got to university and saw a bit more of life. And go to university she would, and on the due date, if her elder sister had anything to do with it.

Suddenly there came a thought Brooke had been too disturbed to consider before. What was Jourdain Marchais' role in all this?

When Stephanie had thought herself in love before, that love had always been returned. The boys she had previously taken a shine to had seemed to be forever either on the phone, or camped out on their doorstep. But Jourdain Marchais was not a boy, but a man—and if Stephanie's description of him was accurate, a sophisticated man of the world at that!

Oh dear, thought Brooke, panic of her own starting to bite. The very fact that Jourdain Marchais ran a successful business enterprise in Paris as well as keeping an eye on his estate in Normandy spoke of his having left the schoolroom long since! Would any man of his alleged sophistication fall in love with a girlish, immature eighteen-year-old? Panic began to spiral at the thought that followed. Had Jourdain Marchais led Stephanie on to believe he loved her, purely for his own ends?

Quickly Brooke scanned again what Stephanie had written, but nowhere could she find any indication that Jourdain Marchais had told Stephanie that he loved her. Which had to mean that he had not. Had he done so, her young and impetuous sister would surely not have left that bit out.

That did not make Brooke feel any more at ease. What did go some way to quieten her agitation, however, was the memory of the letter from the Frenchman to her father, in which he stated his agreement to take Stephanie into his château home until her university term began.

Jourdain Marchais had written that the arrangement would be of advantage to them both, Brooke recalled.

His sister, Madame Rostang, was expecting her husband to join them later and would be holidaying at the château throughout Stephanie's stay, with her daughter, Mélisande. Mélisande, his letter had gone on, was the same age as Stephanie, and she was looking forward to having a holiday companion on whom she could practise her English.

Madame Rostang and Mélisande were indeed at the château. That was borne out by the letter Stephanie had written a week after she had arrived in Normandy. If that one and only letter had also made mention that her host was a bachelor, then neither Brooke nor her father had thought very much about it. Aside from a reference to her host having to go to Paris to keep an eye on his business interests, and how marvellous Normandy was, the best part of what Stephanie had penned had been about Mélisande and her French chic.

Brooke's anxiety was somewhat lessened when she recalled that Madame Rostang was at the Château Marchais. With a daughter the same age she was bound to act as a fine chaperon to Stephanie. Brooke pondered what to do.

To write and tell Stephanie to come home immediately would do no good. Brooke knew in advance that there was nothing more guaranteed to see her sister adopt a defiant attitude than to write to her in such vein.

Fleetingly she thought of ringing her father to ask his advice, but decided against it. With his promotion interview scheduled for Thursday, he was already starting to get uptight. The last thing he needed just now was for Stephanie to upset the applecart.

Only when it came to Brooke that he was going to have to know anyway, since there was no way she could withhold Stephanie's letter, did she realise she could just not sit there doing nothing until he came home that night. There must be something she could do to negate his shock when he read what Stephanie had written.

She glanced at the letter again, and felt angry with Stephanie. She had written herself to tell her the wonderful news of their father's second chance for promotion. It was too bad, Brooke thought, that she should be so careless. The last thing he needed to have on his mind just now was her 'wonderful news'.

Suddenly something about the headed notepaper she held pushed momentarily Brooke's crossness with her sister to one side. All at once the telephone number of the Château Marchais jumped out at her. As suddenly, she had the answer to what she must do.

In the hope of having something to tell her father which would save him from going frantic when he came home, Brooke went to the phone.

She strove for all the calm she could muster when, after some initial difficulty, the number finally started to ring.

Maths had been her subject at school, and it was brought home again what a duffer she was with languages when a voice answered, and she could not understand a word of what was said.

'I don't speak French,' she quickly told the voice at the other end. Then fearing he might not comprehend her language either, she enquired, *'Parlez-vous anglais?'*

'Mais oui,' came the reply. Then, in perfect English, though with a charm which cancelled out her initial relief, 'What would you like to speak about?' he asked.

Oh, grief, thought Brooke, with suspicion growing as to whom she was speaking. That charm alone would send Stephanie all gooey-eyed!

'You are—Monsieur Jourdain Marchais?' she asked, her tone turning cool lest he should think that here was another English miss ready to swoon.

There was a moment's pause, and although a degree of

polite charm was still in his voice, he seemed more distant than he had been, when he replied, 'Jourdain Marchais at your service, Mademoiselle . . .?'

Irked that unless he was used to unknown English women ringing his home he must know full well who she was—the Mademoiselle, not Madame, confirming it— Brooke endeavoured to be as polite as he.

'I'm Brooke Farringdon, Stephanie's sister,' she told him. Loyalty to her sister decreed that she could not breathe a word to him of the worrying letter. Thought of that letter, though, had her voice cool again when she asked, 'May I speak with Stephanie please, *monsieur*?'

'I wish it were so, *mademoiselle*,' he drawled. There was a suggestion in his tone, she thought, that he had grown bored with talking to her—either that, or her cool manner was getting across and he did not care too much for it. 'Your sister is not in at the moment,' he went on. 'However, if you have some urgent message . . .'

'Stephanie is out with Mélisande?' Brooke cut in, her anxiety slightly eased to know that Stephanie was not constantly by his side, but was more often with Mélisande. Seconds later, that ease shortlived, Brooke's anxiety was to shoot into overdrive.

'Unfortunately Henri, Mélisande's father, was taken ill a few days ago,' Jourdain Marchais, still polite, informed her. 'Mélisande and her mother have left my home to be near him.'

Brooke's natural sensitivity made it instinctive to enquire into Monsieur Rostang's health at the present time. She was halfway there with her good wishes for his speedy recovery, when she stopped dead. Suddenly it dawned on her that any quieting thought of Madame Rostang being at the château to chaperon Stephanie had just been declared null and void. Monsieur Rostang's good health was the furthest thing from Brooke's mind then.

'Stephanie—she's still at the château, with you?' she asked, unable to hold down her alarm.

'Of course,' came the stiff reply. 'It was what I agreed with your father, was it not?'

'But . . .'

'Oh, I see,' Jourdain Marchais broke in. Quite obviously he had picked up her alarm, though not the correct reason for it, when he told her, as if to lessen her fears, 'Stephanie is well, and is happy here. She has made no mention of missing Mélisande,' he assured her, 'and appears quite content with my sole company.'

'You're saying—that Stephanie has no other company in your home but yourself, *monsieur*?' Brooke enquired carefully, not liking what she was hearing one little bit, but trying with all she had to remain polite.

'Naturally, there are the servants,' he answered, 'but your sister's—affections—do not lie with domestic matters, I think.'

To Brooke's worried mind, when he appeared as familiar with her language as his own, his use of the word 'affections' had been deliberate. From that one word, she became certain that he was mocking her, and suspicion grew that Stephanie's crush was not one-sided. Something, she felt positive, was definitely going on between the two of them.

'I do not think, *monsieur*,' she said, straining to stay polite; her loyalty to Stephanie under threat as she searched for some tactful way to tell him that she must come home, 'that it is—quite—er—proper that my sister should live alone with you in your home.'

Her piece said, her message put across, Brooke waited for his reply. She did not have to wait long. To her utter astonishment, it was not with words which he immediately replied, but—laughter!

She was stupefied, amazed he should find what she had said so highly amusing. It put paid to any attempt on her part to continue the conversation in dignified politeness.

'I'm glad you find the situation so entertaining, *monsieur*,' she told him coldly. 'But . . .'

Amusement was still in his voice when he butted in, 'I did understand you correctly? You *did* say you were Stephanie's sister?'

'I did,' she confirmed sharply, but when nothing but silence came from him, she felt compelled to enquire disagreeably, 'why do you ask?'

'Stephanie tells me her sister is twenty-two,' he replied. 'Yet it struck me that you sound more like a grandmother than a sister.' And not content with that, he enquired, laughter in his voice even if he was now holding it in check, 'Has no one told you, *mademoiselle*, that we are now in the latter half of the twentieth century?'

The cool cheek of the man! How *dared* he make fun of her! Rattled that he should dare to suggest she sounded like Stephanie's grandmother, only by the skin of her teeth did Brooke refrain from hurling something cutting and unpleasant down the line.

'This may be the latter half of the twentieth century, *monsieur*, she said, her voice tight from the restraint she was using, 'but here in England we tend to care what happens to our young people.'

That took the amusement out of his voice, Brooke heard with some degree of satisfaction. For his tone was cold, and not without a touch of aggression, when he rapped,

'You suggest that in my country we have no regard for our young people?'

'I suggest, *monsieur*,' she replied, with no intention

whatsoever of wasting her phone call arguing the toss with him, 'that you tell my sister she's to come home immediately.'

He did not like her uppity manner, she soon learned, for he grated imperiously, 'Your suggestion, *mademoiselle*, sounds to me very much like a command.'

'Read it which way you like,' she replied, not liking his arrogant way of talking either. 'I want my sister back in England without delay,' she told him haughtily.

Brooke was to see later that she should have realised *that* was just not the way to speak to a descendant of one of the noble houses of France. But no one had ever annoyed her as much as this Frenchman. Even so, she was totally unprepared when, with an arrogance that beat her haughtiness into a cocked hat, he saw no reason to keep up a pretence of politeness and told her bluntly,

'I take orders from no one. If you want your sister home so badly, Mademoiselle Farringdon, then *I* suggest you come and get her.' With that, he had put the phone down.

A couple of hours later Brooke was still smarting from Jourdain Marchais' suggestion that he thought her a throwback from the last century. Dislike of the Frenchman was a fact in her mind, but she still did not know what she was going to do about Stephanie.

Irritatingly, her conversation with Jourdain Marchais kept returning. Drat the man, she thought crossly, but she was certain he would not send her sister home.

Thoughts of his charm—until he had seen her request as an attempt to boss him around—mixed in with thoughts that it was doubtful he would tell Stephanie that she had telephoned at all. Was it likely he would do anything to spoil whatever was going on by telling her her sister was worried about her? Oh, what was she going to do about Stephanie?

It was sheer desperation in the end that showed Brooke what she must do. When the thought 'whatever was going on' triggered off her imagination into alarming bounds, she knew she would not know another moment's peace until Stephanie was safely home.

She had thought she could not withhold Stephanie's letter from her father. But since his peace of mind would be shattered too if he saw that letter, Brooke knew that she could. This last chance of promotion was so important to him. It was vital he should be free of worry—vital, she thought, that he should concentrate solely on doing well at that promotion panel on Thursday.

Clearly Brooke remembered Jourdain Marchais' arrogant, 'If you want your sister home so badly, Mademoiselle Farringdon, then *I* suggest you come and get her.' The light of battle entered her eyes. Damn it, she would! With luck, Thursday would see both her and Stephanie back in England.

The ferry which transported Brooke from England to France the following afternoon took four hours. It was ample time in which to mug up on a road map of Normandy, and in which to relive everything that had taken place.

What she was going to say to her father had troubled her greatly. To make her feel more guilty than ever, he could not have been more enthusiastic when, acquainted with how she thought she might take a short holiday before she began her secretarial course, he had replied warmly,

'I've been telling you for ages it's time you thought of yourself for a change. You'll have to get a move on, though, if you want to be there and back before your term starts. Any idea where you'd like to go?'

'I—er—thought I might use the Austin and take a drive around Normandy,' she brought out hesitantly. 'Stephanie seems to think it's pretty marvellous, and . . .' She was saved from going into a laboured explanation, when he exclaimed,

'That's a splendid idea! You could look her up while you're there.' And Brooke squirmed with guilt, as he added, 'It's ages since we had a letter from her—she could be getting up to all sorts of mischief, for all we know.'

Brooke did what she could in the way of a smile. Then, that hurdle over, her father, without realising it, again helped her out. It was his view, knowing that she would think she had to stay at home to look after him, when he remarked, on seeing the rain lashing the windows, that if Steven was having the same weather on his camping holiday, he might well return early.

'Perhaps I'd better go tomorrow,' she offered tentatively.

'Better the deed, better the day—or something,' Alec Farringdon grinned.

Amazed that, save for her conscience, it had all been so easy, Brooke was in her room putting the few things she thought she would need into an overnight bag, when her father popped his head around the door.

'Oh no,' he said. 'You're going away for a fortnight, Brooke.' In next to no time he had exchanged the small holdall for a large suitcase. 'You just go and enjoy yourself, and don't worry about me—or Steven, for that matter. Come to think of it,' he added, as he stood while she began to fill the case, 'that young man would probably think it a hoot if he has to camp out on some waterlogged field.'

As in England, it was pouring down with rain when the ferry docked at Cherbourg. But the weather conditions were the least of Brooke's worries. It was one thing to come to France to bring Stephanie home, but quite another if Stephanie, at her most self-willed, refused point blank to come.

Mindful that for the first time ever she would be driving on the opposite side of the road, Brooke concentrated hard as she set the car toward the hamlet of Ecartéville where Jourdain Marchais had his home.

Her lack of French made her fearful of losing her way and of not being able to make herself understood should she have to stop for directions. Luck and good road signs were with her, however, and after about an hour and a half of solid concentrated driving, she saw a road sign proclaiming 'Ecartéville'.

She followed the sign, and only then relaxed sufficiently for her good-mannered conscience to prick that maybe she should have telephoned to say she was on her way. She shrugged the thought away. Jourdain Marchais had told her arrogantly to come, so he could have no objection when she arrived unannounced on his doorstep.

Her eyes alert for any building which might be termed a château, she drove at a snail's pace. Here and there she came across the occasional isolated house, but could see no sign of anything more imposing.

She had just cleared a twisting, winding lane, when in the distance she espied a large building which she thought looked promising.

Butterflies started to churn as she turned the car towards the yellow-stoned L-shaped building, and thought of the reception that awaited her. But as she steered her way around well-kept gardens and went up a long drive and into a forecourt, Brooke forgot her worries for a moment. For the château, with its French equivalent of long Georgian windows, was, she thought, truly beautiful.

Her eyes full of admiration, she braked and stepped from the car. Then she wondered if she had got it wrong. Somehow she had expected to see turrets and a suggestion of some ancient castle, but there was none. The structure before her, lovely as it was, bore not a trace of a turret, and was two-storied with a high skylighted roof and tall chimneys. It could well not be the château after all.

Despondency started to set in at the thought that she might have to get back into the car and drive around for an age, when suddenly a tall man coming from a door to the left of the building caught her eye.

Had it been in her mind to go across and trot out her '*Parlez-vous anglais?*' recognition of the blonde with him, her hair only a few shades darker than her own light blonde hair, stopped her.

Brooke knew she had no need to ask the young blonde if she spoke English. Nor, if her suspicion was correct, would she need to ask the same question of the tall dark-haired man who smiled down at the eager young face turned up to him. She knew he could speak English. This had to be the Château Marchais. And, if she was not mistaken, *he* was none other than the arrogant Jourdain Marchais.

Protective instinct grabbed her when, neither of the two having yet seen her, the man placed a hand on Stephanie's arm as if to guide her off in some direction. Then Brooke went smartly forward.

Because Stephanie had her back to her, it was Jourdain Marchais, glancing over to where she approached, who saw her first. Brooke saw his expression register a cool kind of interest as she neared, and strove hard for all the calm she could find.

That cool steady unwavering gaze stayed on her when Brooke halted, within a yard or two of them. It seemed

Jourdain Marchais had no ambition other than to wait for her to state her business. Before she could say a word, however, Stephanie became aware that her companion had been sidetracked.

The smile she wore for him was still on her pretty face when she half turned to see what detained him. Then abruptly she jerked the rest of the way round, her look changing to one of absolute horror.

There was no doubt in Brooke's mind that Stephanie, for one, did not want her at the château. For her voice was utterly appalled when, with not a smile of welcome about her she snapped, 'Why did *you* have to come?'

CHAPTER TWO

HER calm under siege to be spoken to so, and in front of the arrogant Frenchman, Brooke was saved from making any reply when he addressed Stephanie in a fast volley of French. When Stephanie, her look sulky, replied in a quick flow of his own tongue, Brooke felt like slapping the pair of them.

'So,' Jourdain Marchais turned to her, amusement in his eyes, his tone mocking, 'you are Mademoiselle Brooke Farringdon, Stephanie's watchdog, *n'est-ce pas*?'

Watchdog! Startled, Brooke looked from one to the other, and had the uncanniest feeling that Stephanie had just called her by that name. Faintly murderous instincts started to stir in her, but from Stephanie's 'I don't give a damn' expression, experience told her that her sister was best ignored for the moment.

'The very same,' Brooke forced out between her teeth, along with a smile. She held out her hand and noted, as they shook hands, that he appeared to be somewhere in the region of thirty-five. 'I'm taking a short holiday in the area,' she went on politely, and borrowed her father's line, 'I thought, since I was so near, that I might look my sister up.'

'*Eh bien*, it is unthinkable you should be so near, and not pay Stephanie a call,' he remarked. 'Just as it is unthinkable,' he went on, his mocking grey glance leaving his study of her clear creamy complexion to look steadily into her sea-green eyes, 'that you should stay anywhere while you are in *Normandie*, but in my home.'

They were fencing, Brooke knew that as she noted that

28

he must have been fairly near the front when good looks had been handed out. But she had not crossed the Channel and arrived at the château merely to allow the embarrassment of seeming to have angled for an invitation of a bed for the night to sink her.

'How very kind of you, *monsieur*,' she accepted. For all it appeared he was a man who enjoyed life to the full, she could see no trace of dissipation on him.

'My pleasure, *mademoiselle*,' he replied. 'I will instruct my housekeeper to have a room made ready for you. Meantime, if you will give me your keys, I will have your car garaged, and Stephanie can take you to the *salon* for some refreshment.'

She handed him the keys which dangled from her left hand while Stephanie gave forth in French, her tone complaining, Brooke thought. Jourdain Marchais answered her in the same language. Then, when he knew very well that her French was more or less limited to '*parlez-vous anglais?*,' he transferred his look to Brooke, and asked,

'*Parlez-vous français, mademoiselle?*'

'Apart from a word here and there, I'm afraid I don't,' she answered, and knew, because she had already told him that over the phone, that he had said nothing to Stephanie about her telephone call.

'Stephanie has just reminded me how we were going to take advantage of a break between rain showers to take a short walk,' Jourdain Marchais translated, as if he thought it impolite not to now he was acquainted with her lack of French vocabulary. 'But I'm sure you must have much to talk of together,' he added smoothly as he turned to the building.

Brooke caught Stephanie's hostile glance which told her she would much prefer to walk with Jourdain than sit in the *salon* catching up on all the news. But to show that any idea of a walk was at an end, their host opened the door he and Stephanie had come through and stood back waiting for them to precede him.

With Jordain at the rear, Brooke followed a reluctant Stephanie along a narrow hall, which turned off into a much wider hall. It was here that Jourdain Marchais left them with a pleasant, 'I shall look forward to seeing you both at dinner.'

Stephanie, plainly in no mood to sit anywhere taking refreshment with her sister, informed her, 'I'm going up to my room.' Doggedly, Brooke went after her.

Experience told her that Stephanie in an uncommunicative sulky mood was best left alone. But Stephanie could keep it up for a week, and Brooke had every intention of taking her back with her on the ferry tomorrow.

Determined to break down the barriers Stephanie had erected, she followed her into a superb bedroom and closed the door. Whereupon Stephanie's frustration overcame her fit of sulks. 'Why have you come?' she brazened.

'You need to ask?' Brooke was quite well aware that her sister had worked out that she was there in direct response to her letter.

'Good God!' Stephanie exclaimed. 'Just how old do you think I am?'

'If you want to be treated as an adult, you should start acting like one,' Brooke told her a shade sharply.

'Oh, my God!' her sister groaned insolently—Brooke was used to counting up to ten. 'Did Daddy send you?' she questioned hostilely.

'No,' Brooke replied, in the hope that Stephanie would see why she had withheld her letter, 'I didn't show him your letter. He doesn't kn . . .'

'You didn't show . . .' Surprise that she should do

anything in any way underhand made Stephanie break off. 'Well, you might just as well have done,' she was quick to bounce back. 'He's going to have to know sooner or later that I'm not going to university.'

'He ...' Brooke began, then had a sudden flash of insight. 'Oh, Stephanie love,' she said gently, 'I know you're nervous about going to York, but so are ...'

'Nervous? Oh, for crying out loud!' Stephanie exclaimed exasperatedly. 'The only reason I don't want to leave France is that I want to stay here with Jourdain.' Brooke opened her mouth, but Stephanie was surging on. 'So if you've come to try and get me to change my mind, you could have saved yourself the bother. I'm not *going* to university.' She was adamant. 'I'm staying here with Jourdain, who loves me, as I love him.'

'He loves you?' Brooke's protective instincts were out with a vengeance as she recalled from her one sight of him that he looked to be every bit the man of the world which Stephanie's letter had indicated. 'Has he told you he loves you?' she asked urgently, afraid Stephanie was so besotted that she stood no chance of seeing through him if he was just leading her on for his own despicable reasons.

Her panic quietened marginally when Stephanie hesitated. 'Not in so many words,' she owned. 'But he does love me, I just know he does.'

Oh, Stephanie, Stephanie! Brooke mourned silently, and knew, hate it though she might, that she could not baulk this issue. She was going to have to shatter her sister's rose-coloured dreams. Aside from the tremendous hurt her young sister was going to feel when it all came to grief, Stephanie's whole future was at stake.

Her voice was as calm as she could make it when she asked quietly, 'You don't think he intends to marry you, do you, Stephanie?'

'*Marry me!*' The astonished exclamation made it
obvious that she had not got round to thinking in terms of
Jourdain Marchais marrying her. But any small comfort
that brought Brooke did not last. Stephanie made her feel
panic-stricken inside again, when adopting an air of
bravado, Stephanie asked coolly, 'Who wants marriage?'

Brooke hung grimly on to both her patience and her
outward show of calm. 'Then what is it you do want?' she
asked.

Her sister's reply was angry, insolent, and immediate.
'Oh, for God's sake, Brooke,' she retorted, 'grow up!'

The implication behind the angry words that, since she
had been in France, Stephanie herself had 'grown up'
shook Brooke rigid. She hated herself for the question,
but it was something else which she felt she could just not
duck.

'Are you saying,' she began slowly, 'that you and
Jourdain Marchais—have been . . .' The word 'lovers'
never got uttered, for just then a tap on the door heralded
the arrival of a woman of about fifty, smartly dressed in
black.

Stephanie's, 'What do you think?' floated in the air,
and while Brooke was too stunned to know what to think
any more, Stephanie turned to converse with the woman
who had just come in. Then she introduced her as the
housekeeper, Madame Lasserre, and told Brooke that
Madame Lasserre was waiting for her to inspect the
room which had been prepared for her.

Left with little option, if she did not want the
housekeeper to know that things were far from agreeable
between her and her sister, Brooke followed Madame
Lasserre to the next-door room.

As Brooke's eyes flicked from the ceiling-to-floor
dusky pink velvet curtains, looped artistically back by
pink brocade, her worries faded for a few moments.

'Why, it's lovely!' she breathed, her eyes coming away from the matching bedspread.

'You like?' enquired Madame Lasserre, moving over the wall-to-wall cream-coloured carpet, pleasure in her face as she took in Brooke's delighted expression.

'Very much,' Brooke murmured, and asked, 'you speak English, Madame Lasserre?'

'Only—little,' the housekeeper replied. 'If you—speak slow.'

Madame Lasserre stayed with her for a few minutes, and it transpired that Brooke's French was about on a par with the housekeeper's English.

By a joint effort of back-to-front French and back-to-front English Brooke thought she had conveyed that she would be more than comfortable in the room she had been given; and that she had understood that someone called Emilie would bring her some refreshment. Brooke tried to get across that she did not wish to be a nuisance to anyone, then Madame Lasserre departed to attend to other matters.

Brooke spotted that whoever had garaged her car must have used the keys to extract her case from the boot too. For round at the other side of the bed was not only her case, but her car keys as well.

But she had more important matters on her mind. She had only just started re-living her recent conversation with Stephanie and was wondering if her sister, as was not unknown, was merely winding her up for the pure hell of it, when a pretty dark-haired girl arrived with a tea tray.

'Emilie?' she enquired, pleased to know she had comprehended Madame Lasserre correctly, as she observed the finest china set out on the tray.

'Oui, mademoiselle,' the girl replied, and with a sweet smile she moved to set the tray down.

'Parlez-vous anglais?' Brooke enquired, unblushing at her dreadful accent. She discovered that Emilie did not speak English, and was forced to terminate a non-conversation with a smile of her own and a, *'Merci, Emilie.'*

She poured herself a cup of tea, but was too keyed up to have an appetite for any of the pastries daintly arranged on a plate. If Stephanie was deliberately alarming her purely for the sake of it, she had succeeded. Brooke cared for her, and, while she might concede that she could be a shade over-protective, wasn't that only natural? No one could have sat up nights with Stephanie in fear that at any moment she might not draw another breath and not be touched by an over-protective feeling.

She had said Jourdain Marchais loved her, but did he? Somehow Brooke just could not believe it. He was a man with a mature outlook. Could he genuinely be in love with Stephanie, who was intelligent enough to make up for lost time and gain a place at university, yet at the same time was immature and so utterly featherbrained?

An hour later Brooke was still debating. At one stage she had almost gone to have another try at putting some sense into her sister's head. The certainty that she would find her unco-operative had held her back—besides, she needed to think.

Brooke had just started to face the fact that her hopes of taking her sister home tomorrow appeared slimmer than she had imagined, when the most appalling thought suddenly struck her. Stephanie was adamant about not leaving France. Which meant, since Brooke was equally adamant about not returning to their Cheltenham home without her, that she would have to stay too!

Oh dear, she thought wearily, and positively hated the idea of spending more than one night under Jourdain Marchais' roof—even if he had declared she should stay nowhere else while she was in Normandy.

A sharp image of her good-looking, mocking host, appeared in her mind's eye. Quickly she banished it and tried for some clear-headed thinking. But, having ferreted away at the subject so much, she started to grow confused, and only one clear fact emerged. Short of dragging Stephanie out of the château, into her car, and on to the ferry, she had no alternative but to stay too. She would hate it, but there was no other answer.

Brooke went to unpack her case. It might go against the grain to have to accept Jourdain Marchais' hospitality, but Stephanie was more important than ill-at-ease pride.

She would accept dinner at his table too—what better way to observe him and Stephanie together? What better way, since just thinking about it brought confusion, to find out just what that man felt for her sister?

By seven-thirty, Brooke had bathed, applied a light covering of make-up, and was wearing a dress of ice-blue linen. She was in the act of combing her hair when Stephanie came to her room.

One look at her hostile expression as Brooke swung round on the dressing-table stool was enough to tell her that Stephanie was still full of resentment. That was before she opened her pretty mouth to state coldly,

'I've only come to tell you that Jourdain and I usually have a drink in the *salon* before dinner. If you have to, you can join us later,' she added insolently.

Brooke ignored her rudeness. 'Thank you, Stephanie,' she replied calmly.

For all she seemed in a hurry to join Jourdain, Stephanie did not immediately depart. While Brooke was ready to seize any opportunity to suggest she might fancy a ferry ride tomorrow, she knew that to say anything of the sort would only succeed in making her sister more antagonistic than ever.

'Was that all you came in for?' she asked instead, hoping Stephanie had adjusted to her being at the château, and might want to confide. 'Is there anything troubling you, Stephanie?' she probed gently.

'The only thing troubling me,' Stephanie snapped, 'is you! I swear it, Brooke,' she went on, her voice rising, 'if you do anything to spoil this for me, then I'll—I'll . . . kill myself!'

Brooke sighed at the great gulf which had appeared between them in the space of time since she had seen her last. Stephanie's dramatics she took in her stride.

'You know, Stephanie,' she said calmly, aware she was waiting for her sister to react to her dramatic statement, 'I can't help thinking that maybe RADA would have been a more suitable training ground for your talents.'

'Since I've no intention of attending the Royal Academy of Dramatic Art or the University of York either,' Stephanie retorted on a burst of frustrated temper, 'it makes no difference.'

With a toss of her blonde curls she flounced out, and Brooke, with her thoughts more on her sister than on what she was doing, turned back to the mirror to run a comb through her short blonde hair. She observed without much interest the unfussy style, its side parting, and how her hair curtained all the same length down the sides of her face to curve very slightly under of its own accord at the ends.

Stephanie, who could be the dearest girl when everything was going well with her world, was still very much on her mind when she left her room. Were those three years of illness responsible for Stephanie being an emotionally late developer? she wondered.

She had started to descend the stairs when one truth suddenly jumped out and turned all her attempts at logical thinking upside down. When it came to emotional development, Stephanie, with her impetuous loves and hates, was streets ahead of Brooke herself. Already Stephanie had been in love several times, while she, at twenty-two, had not the first idea what it felt like!

The sound of Stephanie laughing broke through her winded thoughts and led her to the *salon*, where, apart from a flicked glance at her, Stephanie had eyes for no one but her host. But the amusement in Jourdain Marchais' glance as he turned to her told Brooke that, while she might be emotionally lacking in the love department, her hate vibes were working overtime.

'Ah, *mademoiselle*,' he murmured, 'I was beginning to think you a figment of my imagination.'

From between her teeth, Brooke forced a cool, 'I'm sorry if I'm late.'

'No matter,' he smiled. 'You are here now. And your father must be the proudest man to have not one but two very lovely daughters,' he added, his charm encompassing Stephanie too.

Brooke knew she had inherited her mother's fine aristocratic features, but no one had ever called her lovely before. Which had to be the reason, she thought, for the surprising feeling of pleasure she experienced. She flicked a glance towards Stephanie, but seeing her sister's obvious pleasure at being called lovely, she realised that she too could be wearing that self-same look. Brooke pulled herself together severely. Goodness, she thought, he had me almost as ga-ga as Stephanie for a moment there!

'May I suggest the same light sherry for you as for Stephanie?' Jourdain Marchais broke through her determination not to be caught napping a second time.

'Nothing for me, *monsieur*,' she refused politely, her dislike of him strengthened by his assumption that, like her sister, she was unused to strong drink—even if that assumption was correct.

'Madame Lasserre will have dinner ready now, anyway,' cut in Stephanie. 'I wonder what we have for dinner tonight, Jourdain.'

'You are hungry?' he enquired, his manner to her sister teasing, Brooke observed.

'Starving!' Stephanie declared, and moved to position herself between them.

'Then we shall rectify your hunger without further delay,' he replied, and escorted them from the *salon* to the *salle-à-manger*.

The dining room was as elegant and as tasteful as any of the other rooms Brooke had been in. Placed opposite her host, with Stephanie next to him, she felt she could not be better situated to witness any telltale look which might flicker between them. That Jourdain Marchais had as full a view of her, and could fully observe her if he wished, mattered not a jot to Brooke.

Their host was a good conversationalist she discovered, as a salmon mousse starter was demolished. He allowed no uncomfortable silences, nor would he allow Stephanie to lapse into the language she had come to France to perfect. For when Stephanie, ignoring Brooke, turned her face to him and gave forth in French, he told her in her own tongue, but with an accompanying smile,

'We will speak English in front of your sister, *petite*.'

That smile! That charm, Brooke thought in disgust. Without a glimmer of a sulk at having her bad manners mildly rebuked, Stephanie's reply was to beam a smile back at him.

Brooke glanced from them to the grace of the room, and knew that the beauty of it would soon get to her if she let it. Then she looked down to her empty plate, raising her head to find a pair of cool steady grey eyes watching her.

Pride, which demanded that he should have no cause to rebuke her lack of manners, meant that all the conversation should not be left to him, and made her say the first thing to come into her head.

'Does Madame Lasserre do the cooking, *monsieur*?' she asked.

He nodded. 'You enjoyed the mousse?'

'Very much,' she replied politely, and was saved from searching for another conversation piece when that lady wheeled in the second course herself.

Brooke found that she had no need to seek a fresh topic, for Jourdain Marchais kept the conversational ball rolling by referring to her own culinary skills.

'Stephanie tells me you also are a master in the kitchen,' he murmured, with what Brooke decided was another basinful of French flattery.

'I wouldn't say that,' she denied, while she wondered what other snippets about their home life Stephanie had dropped. Although she was certain she was immune to Jourdain Marchais' charm, Brooke nevertheless found she had a natural smile of humour on her mouth, when she added, 'And I certainly wouldn't dare to say it in France, when the whole world knows that French chefs reign supreme.'

Oh grief, she thought, the minute the words were out, it must be catching—she had sounded every bit as flattering as he!

'You enjoy your work as the homemaker?' he asked, the curve on his mouth letting her know she had amused him.

A flicker of irritation with him almost had her retorting, 'Somebody has to do it', but the calm of many years' practice came to her aid. 'It has its own reward,' she answered.

'A happy home?' he suggested, seeming to know she had not been talking of financial gain. That was to his credit, Brooke thought, although she was unimpressed.

'I . . .' she hesitated. Was their home a happy one? Given an occasional slanging match between the twins, she hoped it was happy. She flicked a glance to Stephanie and, seeing she looked a little petulant at having no part in this conversation, included her, when she replied, 'Perhaps Stephanie would be the best person to answer that question.'

'Then I already have the answer,' he replied. 'Stephanie has been a ray of sunshine ever since the moment she arrived.' While Stephanie perked up to positively glow, Jourdain left Brooke with only enough time to think, Goodness, has she been on her best behaviour? before adding, 'It naturally follows that for her to be so happy, her home background must also be happy.'

Brooke could think of a couple of reasons for her sister's sunny temperament since she had been at the château. She had been far from sunny until—with Brooke's connivance—her father had agreed to let her come to France. So why would Stephanie be anything but on top of the world from the moment of setting her feet on French soil? There was no need to look beyond her declaration that she loved Jourdain Marchais, either, to know why she was still showing him her sunny side. Stephanie wanted Jourdain to be in love with her; as yet, he had not told her what he felt.

The next course had been served when it occurred to Brooke that if Stephanie was still in the dark about Jourdain's feelings, then so was she. She had watched and observed discreetly, but, while it was obvious that Stephanie hung on his every word, Brooke had not been able to pick up from Jourdain any sign of attachment for her sister. Which could mean that he was being too clever by half.

The awful thought that, with Jourdain Marchais playing clever devils, she could still be here next week and still be no further forward, sent her into a mild panic. It caused her to leave her veiled study of her host and, since she wanted to take Stephanie back to England with her as soon as possible, concentrate solely on her.

'You received my letter telling you about Father's chance of promotion?' she went to work.

'Has he had his interview yet?' asked Stephanie with scant interest, more concerned about the man at her side.

'His interview is scheduled for tomorrow,' Brooke refreshed her memory.

'Fancy you coming away from home and leaving him to find his own clean white shirt!' Stephanie was unable to resist the jibe.

Brooke managed to maintain a serene front. But she thanked Jourdain Marchais not at all when, as if he had spotted her quickly concealed hurt, he cut in suddenly,

'Your father is well, I hope?'

'Extremely,' she replied, her tone cool. Then she saw a way to get her meaning across to Stephanie without inviting any more painful jibes in front of a man she barely knew. Her cool tone had gone when she added, 'Stephanie may not have told you, but my father was in such despair when our mother died that his work went to pieces.'

A feeling of being disloyal to her father pricked her, but it was Stephanie's future she was fighting for. Feelings of disloyalty, along with pride, had to take a back seat.

'It would be a blow to any man to lose a much-loved wife,' Jourdain murmured. 'But you were there,' he said, and smiled at her. 'Stephanie has told me how you gave up your studies to stay at home to look after your family.'

Brooke forgot the sincerity in his smile that she had glimpsed for the first time. 'Anyone would have done the same,' she mumbled, niggled that when she wanted to remind Stephanie of their father, Jourdain had taken the conversation away from him.

'But you were only sixteen!'

She was forced to acknowledge that there had been ample time during Stephanie's stay for her to repeat the family history a dozen times or more. 'My father was in despair, as I told you,' she replied, glad to have brought the conversation back to her parent. 'But thank goodness,' she sent her host a smile, 'he's now more the man he was. He so deserves to be happy. And, if life has no more cruel tricks to play, and he does get this promotion, we shall all be very pleased.'

'I wonder how Monsieur Rostang will fare tomorrow,' Stephanie butted in to change the subject, making Brooke's efforts seem like water off a duck's back.

'Monsieur Rostang?' she queried. She had entirely forgotten the existence of a Monsieur Rostang.

'Have you not told your sister how Mélisande's father was taken ill a few days ago?' Jourdain asked Stephanie smoothly.

Recollection came to Brooke and with it the memory that it had been Jourdain Marchais himself who had told her over the telephone that his brother-in-law had been taken ill. In a state of confusion, not knowing if she wanted Stephanie to be aware of her telephone call, she found herself saying,

'I do hope it's nothing serious.'

'Henri will have further tests tomorrow,' Jourdain replied.

Whereupon Stephanie, as though to prove her closeness with Jourdain and his family, got in quickly,

'Madame Rostang suggested I should go with them when she and Mélisande left.'

Brooke took heart that Madame Rostang, if nobody else, seemed to be aware of where the proprieties lay. she felt a prick of annoyance when she caught the quirk of amusement in Jourdain Marchais' expression. It gave her the sensation that he had just read her mind and thought her old-fashioned beyond belief.

'You couldn't very well go with them,' she roused herself to tell Stephanie, holding back from adding that she should have had the sense to see she should have come home straight away. 'Madame Rostang has enough to worry about at the present time, without . . .'

'That's what Jourdain said,' Stephanie chipped in. 'But in any case I couldn't have gone. Not while Jourdain needs my help with his office work.'

'You're doing *office work*!' Brooke exclaimed, staggered. She had no need to search her memory to recall her sister's appalled comments, her 'You'd never get me within a mile of any stuffy office', when she had told her she was hoping to make the grade as a secretary.

'Which reminds me,' Jourdain addressed Stephanie, while Brooke was realising how far gone she must be on the man to help him with his office work so happily, 'you promised to finish the filing when we returned from our "breath of fresh air".'

'Oh!' Stephanie exclaimed, 'I forgot! We never did go for our walk though, did we,' she added with a glance at Brooke whose untimely arrival had put paid to the idea. Proving that she was as impulsive as ever, Stephanie jumped up, and beamed at Jourdain. 'I'll go and do it now,' she said. 'It won't take me half a tick.' Then she was gone.

In the moments that followed the closing of a door somewhere along the hall, Brooke grew convinced that,

since Jourdain Marchais had not told Stephanie the
filing could well wait until tomorrow, he had engineered
her absence. Which was fine by her, Brooke considered.
If he wanted a private word with her, then, in her view, it
was more than time that she said one or two pertinent
things to him.

'Shall we take coffee in the *salon*?' he suggested.
Brooke was in full agreement.

Magically, Madame Lasserre appeared, to follow them
into the *salon* with a tray of coffee. Then she left the
room. Invited to pour, Brooke handed Jourdain his
coffee, and, with her mind on what she wanted to say, she
took hers to an easy chair.

Jourdain took a chair opposite but, ever a man to
annoy her, he annoyed her again when he promptly took
the initiative from her before she could get a word out.

'Tell me, *mademoiselle*,' he said, 'are you always so
tightly controlled?'

His question was the last thing she had expected, and
Brooke's coffee threatened to slop over. 'I beg your
pardon?' she queried coldly, fully conscious that she had
heard him correctly since he spoke English with barely a
trace of accent.

'It is plain there has been friction between you and
your sister,' he replied, her cold tone affecting him not
one whit. 'But while at dinner Stephanie could not
contain her crossness with you, not once did you allow
yourself to show your anger with her.'

Here was someone else with whom she was going to
have to count ten, thought Brooke. 'I see little point,
monsieur, in both Stephanie and me screaming our heads
off at each other,' she told him with cool civility. 'That
would get neither of us anywhere.'

'And the *anywhere* you're determined to go is back to
England—with Stephanie.'

'That's why I'm here,' Brooke replied stonily, and reminded him, 'you suggested yourself that I should "come and get her".'

He inclined his head in agreement, then asked, 'Your father, he knows why you have come to Normandie?'

She felt a shade uncomfortable as she replied, 'My father thinks I've come to Normandy for a holiday. But it will only be a short holiday,' she added quickly. 'I was hoping to go back tomorrow. But Stephanie . . .'

'Is proving a little—difficult?'

'I haven't asked her yet to come with me tomorrow,' Brooke admitted. She was suddenly aware that she had said none of the things she should be saying, and was about to demand to know what the dickens he thought he was playing at. Again he took the initiative from her. This time, in consequence, he all but floored her, when he asked,

'You think *mademoiselle*, you will get her agreement to go with you, by the use of—emotional blackmail?'

'Emotional blackmail!' she exclaimed, staring at him.

'You laboured the point purposely, did you not,' he suggested, 'when you tried to make her see how important it is that your father, after so much sadness, should be happy from now on?'

An honesty Brooke would have preferred not to acknowledge at that moment, forced her to see that Jourdain Marchais' terminology was indeed correct. She *had* stooped to try and use that dreadful tool, emotional blackmail.

'I'll concede you're right,' she owned up. In spite of her wish to stay calm, she had started to feel snappy. 'But I'll use any weapon I can,' she said shortly.

Moments went by when her host appeared to be more arrested by the flicker of angry fire that lit her eyes than he was concerned to make any reply. Then, a master at ruffling her calm, he murmured,

'It's a great pity, *mademoiselle*, you should know so little about young people.'

Her reply was immediate. 'I've looked after *two* young people for the past six years, so I should know something about them!' she exploded. Calm, which was so much a part of her, was hauled back. 'I will grant, though, that you probably know quite a lot about young *women*,' she told him acidly.

To her annoyance, his only reaction to her sarcasm was to show her his perfect teeth in a grin of pure amusement. Her annoyance with him did not lesen when, a second later, he said,

'It is clear you cannot bear to let go the hold you have on young Stephanie's reins.' Certain that he was baiting her, Brooke's mouth compressed. His next remark, however, made her forget every bit of her aggravation with him. 'Cannot you see, *mademoiselle*,' he enquired casually, 'that once the little one is at university, your hold on her reins will have to be severed?'

'You—don't know!' Brooke said faintly, half to herself. And at his look of waiting to be acquainted with that which he did not know, she told him flatly in a stronger voice, 'Stephanie had stated categorically that she had no intention of going to university.'

All amusement left him abruptly, and Brooke took heart that he appeared to regard this news as seriously as she. 'She has told you this?' he questioned sharply.

'Both verbally and in writing,' she confirmed, and thought to add, lest he considered her father uncaring of Stephanie, 'I didn't want to worry my father, so he doesn't know about the letter we received from Stephanie yesterday.'

'This letter—it was the reason for your telephone call?' he asked promptly, revealing to Brooke that there was nothing the matter with the Frenchman's intelligence as he digested her deceit to her father. 'You came so swiftly, not as I thought from concern about her being unchaperoned—it has nothing to do with that—but . . .'

'It has everything to do with that,' Brooke cut in sharply, unconcerned when he started to look a degree arrogant at the suggestion that his moral outlook might be in question. She had been through too much agony of mind to care if he laughed at her again or became mortally offended. She just had to know, when she demanded coldly, 'Tell me plainly, *monsieur*, are you trifling with my sister's affections?'

'Trifling?' The detached look of him as he set his coffee cup and saucer down on a table told her he knew the word and the context in which she had used it—and that he had taken exception to being asked such a question.

His sudden aloof manner was offputting, but Brooke had too much grit to back out now that she had got this far.

'To be more specific,' she persisted, as her coffee cup joined his on the table, 'are you just playing around with my sister, or are you . . .?'

'You dare to ask . . .' Jourdain sliced in, outraged.

'Stephanie's only reason for saying she will not go to university,' Brooke cut straight in, the bit well and truly between her teeth, 'is that she wants to stay here—with you.' She saw he was about to interrupt again, and so quickly that somehow her natural loyalty to her sister got lost, she told him, 'She believes she's in love with you.'

Jourdain Marchais' astonishment, not to mention his amazed silence, told Brooke that this was the first he had heard of it. But as it penetrated that he had neither verbally denied or confirmed anything, she knew she was just not going to go to bed with nothing resolved.

The time had come to try to jolt him into making some sort of admission or denial. For herself, she did not go in for dramatics. But she did not wish to spend another hour in the same ragged demented thought which had been hers since she had opened that letter. Brooke saw no reason why she should not borrow a leaf out of Stephanie's dramatic book.

'Stephanie,' she said, observing she had his full attention, 'is so—gone on you—that she told me quite unequivocaly, that if I do anything to spoil things for her, then . . .' she paused for better effect, '. . . then she will—kill herself.'

His eyes narrowed, though what she expected him to answer, Brooke was uncertain. She was sure, however, that when it came to rubbing her up the wrong way, Jourdain Marchais had no equal. It was a second or two before he replied to her dramatic statement. Then he answered, quite deliberately, she thought,

'It would appear, *mademoiselle*, that you have something of a problem.'

'I know *that*!' she flared, then strove desperately for calm. A modicum of that calm was hers when she suggested more civilly, 'You don't think that perhaps you too have something of a problem, *monsieur*?'

'I, *mademoiselle*?' he enquired politely, his raised eyebrows making it patently obvious that he was surprised she should think the problem in any way his.

Brooke knew then that she would get no help from him. Pride would have made her march from the room without another word, but a stubbornness to fight for Stephanie and her future made Brooke stay exactly where she was.

'Very well, *monsieur*,' she said coldly. 'I accept that the problem is mine alone. Just as I accept that the responsibility for Stephanie and her future wellbeing is mine. But,' acid entered her tones, 'since my father only allowed her to come here in the belief that you were a gentleman ...' her voice faded when she caught a glimpse of fury that flashed briefly to his eyes when, for a second time, she dared to question his honour, '... that you,' she resumed, 'have some small responsibility for her too?'

If her voice was cold, then his was positively arctic, when Jourdain Marchais told her, 'My responsibility is to see that Stephanie is cared for, is well and happy. Can you say that she is not?' he challenged icily.

'She is sublimely happy here,' Brooke admitted. 'But I want her home.'

His arrogant stare told her 'Tough'. She recognised that she had never before met a man who was capable of instantly scattering her calm to the four winds. But she fought to recapture her composure.

She made a fresh attempt to get through to him. 'Stephanie has worked extremely hard to win her place at university. Don't you see, she just cannot be allowed to turn her back on all she has achieved—on her bright future.' The frail grip she had on her calm started to slip once more when she received no answer but a steady stare. 'The least you could do,' she went on, her sea-green eyes once again starting to spark fire, 'would be to tell her that with Madame Rostang and Mélisande gone, it's no longer convenient to have her here.'

Jourdain Marchais looked away from her and appeared to find the coffee pot of interest. But Brooke felt instinctively that he was considering what she had just said rather than idly appreciating his fine china, and her hopes started to rise. Her nerve ends were all anticipation that she had finally got through to him and the smile that came to his face gave her further cause for hope. But that was before he spoke.

'But how can I tell her she must leave, *mademoiselle*?'
he enquired, his smile fading under a look of regret.
'Have I not given your father my word in writing that I
will house his younger daughter until the week before her
university term begins?"

'But Stephanie says she isn't . . .'

Jourdain Marchais ignored her attempted interrup-
tion. 'I could not upon my French honour,' he said,
repaying her for casting doubts on him being a
gentleman, 'break such a promise—least of all to an
Englishman.'

Her hopes were in tatters, and only then did Brooke
realise how much she had offended him by her
disparaging remarks. Yet, just when the irritant of
Jourdain Marchais became a bit too much, and might
have seen her offend him yet again, something new in his
expression told her that he had just thought of something.

'What . . .?' she just had to ask.

'It—might work,' he said slowly, his expression
thoughtful.

'What might work?' she asked eagerly, hoping again
that he had come to see things her way, and that, for all
she had offended his French pride, he might have found
a way to help.

'It might not work,' he cautioned, to her aggravation
delaying to tell her what was on his mind. 'But I'm
willing to give it a try.'

'But it might work?' Brooke pressed, still eager to hear
what he had to say.

'It has occurred to me, since I cannot break my word to
your father—and most definitely since we cannot have
the pretty Stephanie committing suicide—that there may
be a way out of this, while at the same time I retain my
honour.'

'What way?' asked Brooke, her hopes never higher

despite her frustration at being kept on tenterhooks.
'How?' she asked urgently, her expression alive.

'Your eyes mirror your soul,' Jourdain Marchais
remarked, throwing her. 'There is passion in you,
mademoiselle,' he added, when Brooke was all but on the
edge of her chair to know what chance of a solution he
had hit upon. 'A passion which you are at pains to keep
concealed.'

'For goodness' sake!' she exploded—it was just as if he
was dragging it out on purpose!

Jourdain smiled, and murmured, more as if he was
talking to himself than to her, 'Yes, perhaps it will not be
so very difficult for me.'

Brooke took a deep and controlling breath. 'Would you
mind, very much, telling me what it is you're talking
about?' she asked. 'You said there might be a way to
solve my—er—our problem. What way have you found?
What do you intend to do?' she insisted upon knowing
without further delay.

'It is more, I think, a question of what will *we* do,'
Jourdain replied, and, as if he did not intend to miss a
blink of any reaction, he leaned forward in his chair.
'The best way to cure the—infatuation—you say Stephanie has for me,' he told her smoothly, 'can only be,
mademoiselle, for me to pretend to be enamoured of you.'

Shock made Brooke's eyes wide, as she reacted by
abruptly getting up from her chair. Jourdain rose too,
and took a step towards her.

'It has been my experience—with only the occasional
exception,' he threw in coolly, his mouth unsmiling, but
some devilish amusement lurking in the grey eyes that
surveyed her staggered expression, 'that members of
your fair sex show a great deal of pride in these matters.
Stephanie, I am certain, is no exception. Just as I am
certain her pride will have her pretend it is of no

consequence that I am enamoured with you, she will, nevertheless, insist you both return to England. *Naturellement*,' he concluded, while Brooke, stunned, could only stare at him, 'you will have to react—favourably—to my—overtures.'

She was still staring at him as she tried for comprehension. If she had heard correctly, Jourdain Marchais had just said he would pretend to take a fancy to her—a fancy which had to be reciprocated—whereupon Stephanie, her pride in uproar, would want to return voluntarily to England! His honour would then still be intact because he was still prepared to honour his promise to house Stephanie, but could not be held responsible if Stephanie *wanted* to go home. Then Jourdain Marchais could quite cheerfully wave them off!

Brooke was still catching her breath from what he had suggested, when Jourdain stepped closer and placed an arm intimately across her shoulders.

'A little light—dalliance—should be all that is called for,' he bent to murmur in her ear, his action and his words making her too dumbstruck to move a muscle. 'There is one small chance though, *chérie*,' he added softly, a hand coming to tilt up her face so he could see into her eyes, 'but a chance just the same, that I shall have to take you to my bed.'

The first shock he had given her sent Brooke into stunned silence, but the second shock, as what he had just said registered, was the perfect antidote. There was not a thought in her head of Stephanie when, with a shriek of fury, she came out of her shaken silence.

'How *dare* you?' she flew at him, the flame of fury ablaze in her eyes. She was too angry as she pushed him away to note the flicker of admiration his eyes held. She did not miss his amusement though, when, enraged that any man could suggest what he had to her, she shouted,

'You—you—conceited French flirt!' and stormed to the door.

His laugh followed her, mocking her as he told her, 'It is my belief, *mademoiselle*, that you have never yet kissed a man, much less been to bed with one.' He made her so boilingly furious, she just had to turn to fling at him,

'You can bank on it, *monsieur,* that the first time I *do* go to bed with a man, it certainly won't be with you!'

'So you *are* a virgin,' he grinned, apparently unable to contain his humour at having contracted that piece of information from her.

Stumped for anything either brilliant or subtle to slam back, 'Oh, go and take a running jump!' Brooke hurled at him, and shot from the *salon*, to almost cannon into Stephanie on her way in from the other side.

'Where's the fire?' questioned Stephanie, not quick enough to remember she was not friends with her sister.

Brooke did not answer, but went smartly up to her room. Jourdain Marchais was disgusting, disgusting, to make the suggestion he had! she fumed. No gentleman, whatever Jourdain Marchais thought himself, would make a suggestion like that, she silently railed. Mocking devil! she raged against him. Who did he think he was to suggest that he was willing, *if he had to*, to put himself out and take her to his bed!

Never had the controlled person she knew herself to be been turned so upside down. Brooke was still up in arms when, washed and changed into her night things, she climbed into the fourposter bed.

As she put out the light and mentally blasted him to damnation, some of her fury let up as she remembered Stephanie's reply of 'What do you think?' when she had all but asked her sister if she and Jourdain Marchais were lovers.

Brooke thought back to when she had asked him if he

was trifling with her sister. She remembered his aloofness and how offended he had been when she had pressed him to know if he was playing around with Stephanie. And Brooke knew then that the inference in Stephanie's 'What do you think?' was just so much nonsense. Jourdain Marchais and her sister were not lovers—nor did he want Stephanie in his bed.

Hot on the heels of that came her memory of his suggestion that—if he had to—he would take *her* to his bed. Brooke fumed silently. But before she fell into a fitful sleep one very clear fact had emerged. Whatever it was that Stephanie felt for him, Jourdain Marchais would certainly not have suggested what he had, if he had been in love with Stephanie!

CHAPTER THREE

HAD Brooke hoped that the coming of daylight might show her worries to be not so large, then she was doomed to disappointment. For next morning, a new dimension was added. How was she to tell Stephanie that Jourdain Marchais did not love her?

To cause her sister pain was equally painful to Brooke. But, if Stephanie was in the same mood today as yesterday, and Brooke guessed it was pretty certain she would be, then Brooke could not see her being receptive to anything her sister told her. It was certain anyway that Stephanie would not believe her.

Wearily Brooke left her bed and went to the adjoining bathroom, thinking, as she ran her bath, that Stephanie could well dig in her stubborn heels even further when she knew her sister had discussed her with Jourdain.

Experience forewarned her that anything Brooke said at all of that discussion might easily make Stephanie—for the pure perversity of it, if nothing else—more determined than ever to stay in France.

Not that she would tell her anything of that disgusting suggestion Jourdain Marchais had made, Brooke thought, starting to feel angry. Him and his French honour! How honourable to suggest that, in order to save *his* honour, she might have to lose *hers*!

It was bad enough that she had lost her usual control and had nearly yelled at him to go and take a running jump, but her control was all she was going to lose.

The calm which was normally part and parcel of her, threatened to get away again when she left her room with

55

Jourdain Marchais dominating her thoughts. Aware that she was going to need every ounce of calm when Stephanie started to become deliberately obstructive, Brooke ousted him from her mind. Briefly she considered tapping on her sister's door to see if she was ready to go down to breakfast, but decided against it. As yet she had not determined just how much or how little she should tell Stephanie.

At the bottom of the stairs she met the housekeeper who, after greeting her with a pleasant, *'Bonjour, mademoiselle,'* led the way to a small ante-room where Brooke saw that a breakfast setting had been laid for one.

Hoping that Stephanie, who was of her own slender proportions, had not taken up some daft slimming notion, which included not eating breakfast, Brooke tried to get across to Madame Lasserre that she would wait for her sister to join her.

'Mais, Mademoiselle Stephanie 'as eaten the *petit déjeuner,'* the housekeeper replied.

'Stephanie has breakfasted already?' Brooke exclaimed, forgetting to attempt a reply in French, in her surprise that Stephanie, who always had to be prised out of bed in the morning, was up and about before her.

That was not her only surprise. For when, with a similar mixture of French and English as before, Madame Lasserre went on to explain further, Brooke learned with no small astonishment that Mademoiselle Stephanie was hard at work with Monsieur Marchais in his study.

As Brooke tried to conceal her astonishment a maid, introduced by the housekeeper as Grace, came in with fresh croissants. Grace, it appeared, spoke no English, and soon departed. Whereupon, Madame Lasserre, after casting an eye over the table and assuring herself that all was as it should be, left Brooke to eat her breakfast undisturbed.

She was disturbed, though. Her anxieties were taking on mammoth proportions. Here she was, desperate to get Stephanie home, and there was Stephanie, determined to stay put. And for all the help Jourdain Marchais had been last night, Brooke might as well have saved her breath. To hear him tell it he would die before he broke his word of honour to her father, and he had no intention of telling Stephanie her presence was inconvenient.

Thinking over her conversation with Jourdain Marchais, Brooke saw that the only good thing to come out of it was the knowledge that he was neither trifling with Stephanie, nor was he in love with her. Much good it would do to tell Stephanie that he did not love her, Brooke thought glumly, her intention to do just that starting to waver. The very fact that Stephanie, with her aversion to office work, not to mention her dislike of getting up in the morning, was now not only up but hard at work in Jourdain's study, spoke volumes.

Too upset to eat, Brooke drank a cup of coffee and left the room. She was at the bottom of the stairs when she realised that it was more than she could take to go back to her room and sit twiddling her thumbs until Stephanie had finished her 'office work'. Without having to think about it, she knew that her sister would not welcome her going to the study to suggest she accompany her for a walk. Brooke decided to take a look outside.

It was a mild day, and when she stepped from the front door she saw that, although the sky did not look too promising, at least it was not raining.

The beauty of the château struck her again as she strolled across in front of its mellowed brickwork. Could grass really be so green as these perfect lawns?, she wondered, and, strangely, some of her anxiety began to subside. Imagine living here the whole year round, she

found herself thinking. Not that Jourdain lived here
always. According to Stephanie, part of his time was
spent in Paris. She wished he was in Paris now and that
he would stay there. That thought abruptly ended any
brief respite to her worries.

Her footsteps slowed and then stopped. With anxiety
pricking at her again, Brooke didn't notice that she had
stopped where the yellow stone brickwork of the château
ended, or that she stood close to a window. Until a
movement on the other side of the glass drew her
attention to the room beyond. It was a study, she saw,
and the movement which had caught her gaze had been
made by Jourdain Marchais, his face hidden as he leant
over Stephanie who was seated at a desk, as if to explain
some detail to her. How much Stephanie comprehended
of his instruction, Brooke had no idea. But the sight of
the total infatuation on her sister's face as she looked at
him was more than enough to make Brooke quickly
move away.

When she found that her feet had hastened her away
from the building and down the long drive, she was of no
mind to go back.

Hurriedly, as if to put as much distance between her
and the château as possible, Brooke stepped into the lane
at the bottom of the drive. The countryside was green,
picturesque, and very much like England, but she was so
agitated she barely noticed. She was tormented by a new
worry.

Had Jourdain Marchais truly been instructing Stephanie in some detail of work or, aware now of the girl's
infatuation for him—since Brooke herself had told him
about it—was he making capital out of that information?

Brooke was too concerned to linger on the memory of
how offended Jourdain had been at any suggestion that
he was trifling with Stephanie. All she knew as she left

the winding lane and, slowing her pace, walked on, was that her young sister had looked so besotted that she would be an absolute pushover for a man of his worldly ways. Brooke wished quite desperately that she had been able to see the expression on his face. Had it been purely businesslike, or, seeing in that eager young face turned to him, all the encouragement a man could want, had he been luring her on?

Brooke groaned inwardly as her feet took her along the road down which she had motored yesterday. What a nightmare it all was!

Some time later, rain splashing on her face halted her frayed thinking and caused her to stop to get her bearings. It was only then that she realised that not only must she be a mile or so away from the château, but also that she was standing in the middle of a downpour.

A soaking being the least of her troubles, she turned. The summer skirt she had on was already clinging wetly to her legs. If the rain kept up she was going to look a fine bedraggled specimen when she reached the château!

The rain did indeed keep up, but she was spared a long walk. As she reached some crossroads, a sleek dark car appeared from the opposite direction. Jourdain Marchais was at the wheel. The car slowed and was turned around, and in next to no time her host was asking her,

'May I be permitted to give you a lift, *mademoiselle*?'

As she caught his look of amusement at the sorry sight she presented, she nearly told him coldly that she preferred to walk. But, needing to have her mind put at rest about her most recent worry, she accepted his offer with what grace she could.

'I thought you were again going to tell me to take a running jump,' Jourdain murmured, as Brooke climbed soggily in beside him, the quirk at the corner of his mouth making her quite sure she was not going to apologise for her remark of the previous evening.

For the moment she ignored him, though when he did not immediately start up the car, but handed her a large white handkerchief, she took it from him. He was good at being amused at her expense. Perhaps she stood a better chance of being taken seriously if she mopped herself up a bit.

'Thank you,' she said quietly, when, after drying her face, she had dabbed at her hair. Not knowing quite what to do with the wet handkerchief, but certain he wouldn't want to put it back in his pocket, she placed it by the windscreen.

She was confused for a moment, when her eyes went to his face and she saw his attention had been drawn to where the cotton of her shirt was clinging to the curves of her bosom.

His grey eyes did not linger, however, but when they looked into hers, she thought, oddly, that she saw a touch of something strangely gentle in them too. Odder still, that produced in her a feeling of not wanting to be argumentative. She felt her edginess with him start to wane and had the most peculiar feeling of wanting to be at one with him.

That feeling was destined not to last, although his voice was more sympathetic than she had heard it so far, when he said quietly, 'You look tired, Brooke.'

The sound of her Christian name on his tongue for the first time might have made her give in to the empathy of the moment. But suddenly she recalled that it was partly because of him that she looked tired. Had there been no such person as Jourdain Marchais, she would not have lain awake half of last night in fretful worry over Stephanie.

'To be told I look a wreck is all I need, Monsieur Marchais,' she told him formally, to let him know she had no intention of being so friendly as to call him by his first name.

'Ah,' he said, clearly in no way put out, 'you feel a need to—um—fish for compliments, *mademoiselle*?'

'Fish for . . .!' she gasped.

He continued as if she had not spoken. 'Even with your tired eyes and your make-up washed away you are beautiful. And,' he went on, when, struck dumb to hear him say such a thing, Brooke stared wide-eyed at him, 'with bone structure such as yours, beautiful is what you will always be.'

Momentarily she was left with nothing to say, but not for long. Suddenly, the thought occurred to her that, just as Jourdain Marchais' charm was as natural to him as breathing, so was his inability to resist the chance of some small flirtation.

'I commend you on your excellent eyesight, *monsieur*,' Brooke told him sourly. 'But if my suspicions are correct, I'm sure you've said much the same thing to my sister less than an hour ago.'

That took the smile off his face, she noted with satisfaction, when, as blunt as she, and tough with it, he rapped, 'Explain yourself, *mademoiselle*!'

Not certain she liked the stern look she had provoked any better than his amusement, she asked, 'Do you deny, in the light of what I told you of Stephanie's infatuation for you, that it has not crossed your mind to . . .' she had no need to continue, for he was there before her.

Brooke was left to wait for his answer. As if the violence of his feelings caused him to need some sort of action—other than his first choice of choking the life out of her—Jourdain thrust the car into gear and it shot forward.

A moment later, Brooke was to wonder if she had imagined his aggression. As though he had never been in danger of losing his control, he replied to her accusation, and his reply came near to sending her out of control instead.

'Stephanie is a pretty little thing,' he drawled silkily, 'and of age to make her own decisions, is she not?'

'What's that supposed to mean?' shot from Brooke, her throat suddenly dry.

His shrug seemed to say it all, and that was before he stated, 'Did she not come to France to learn—all—she could?' Shock at having her latest fear confirmed kept Brooke silent. Jourdain, with a sideways look at her stunned expression, smiled, and went on, 'What quicker way to cure her infatuation, *mademoiselle*, than to help it run its full course?'

'You can't . . .' she burst out hotly, and was interrupted when, with a shrug of his broad shoulders, Jourdain cut in,

'*Naturellement*, I will honour the offer of a solution I made to you last night, if you prefer I cure her love for me that way.'

The winding lane they were travelling along told Brooke they would soon be at the château. Shaken again into silence, she knew that, when it came to options, she did not have any. Stephanie and her wellbeing were still of prime importance.

'If—if I pretend to—to like you a little,' she managed to get out, 'do I have your word you will make no—overtures—to my sister?'

His smile gone, Jourdain made her wait for her answer until he had pulled up in front of the château. Brooke knew his loss of humour had nothing to do with her intimation that she did not like him, but would pretend to. For he left her in no doubt that he wouldn't enjoy having to honour his offer, as his eyes scanned the face he had minutes before called beautiful, and then brusquely he told her,

'God knows what pleasure I shall find in thawing your English blood, but you have my word.'

She did not wait to hear any more. With no intention of having her English blood thawed, and certainly not by him, she got wordlessly out of the car and hurried indoors.

Brooke spent what was left of the morning in her room. She had a shower, changed into dry clothes and, not at all happy with her deceit, she reached the conclusion that lunch would be soon enough to see Stephanie.

That Stephanie did not come to seek her out was a blessing for once. Even so, the nearer lunchtime came, the more Brooke's stomach started to churn. How on earth was she supposed to act with Jourdain Marchais with Stephanie there? She refused point blank to simper.

It was not Stephanie, but the young maid Grace, who, with the use of sign language, came to tell her that lunch was ready. Brooke needed a few minutes to get herself under control, anticipating that she was going to have to make encouraging noises to any flirtatious remarks Jourdain Marchais made over the lunch table. Then she left her room.

There was to be a brief respite before her acting abilities were tried out, however. For, when Brooke walked into the dining room, although Stephanie was seated at the table, there was no sign of Jourdain Marchais.

'He found you, then?' Stephanie enquired, looking up from her soup. Her manner was not the most affable.

'Who?'

'Jourdain—who else?' Stephanie replied, as Brooke joined her at the table. 'We saw you belting down the drive from the study window. When it came on to rain, Jourdain remembered you weren't wearing a coat and came after you.'

'He came—especially to pick me up?' Brooke asked, startled, having imagined that he must have been on his way to somewhere or other when he had seen her.

Stephanie nodded. 'Did you get wet?' she asked. To Brooke's mind, her look was hopeful.

To have Stephanie still at war with her showed her that today as yesterday she would be as receptive as a brick wall to any suggestion that she accompany Brooke back to England.

'Soaked,' Brooke replied briefly, and was giving her attention to the soup tureen, when good manners instilled by her mother made her hesitate. 'I'd better wait for our host.'

'I shouldn't,' Stephanie replied airily. 'He's out visiting one of the farms. I expect he'll lunch there.'

Brooke ladled out soup, and started to feel more cheerful at the delay in having to respond to any of Jourdain Marchais' overtures. But as she thought about it, that feeling of cheerfulness departed. How on earth were she and her host to test his theory of Stephanie being so piqued she would want to go home, if the three of them were never in the same room together?

She had said goodbye to being able to take Stephanie home that day, and saw any chance of achieving her object tomorrow start to fade too. Brooke mulled her problem over. The second course had been brought to the table when she saw that, if Stephanie was to be made to believe that she too had taken a shine to Jourdain Marchais, it might not be a bad idea, in his absence, to show a little interest in him.

'Does . . .' his name stuck in her throat, '. . . Jourdain,' she made it, 'often lunch out?'

'More often he has his meals with me,' Stephanie replied. Her look and her words were both meant to

imply a closeness of a relationship which just wasn't
there, Brooke saw.

'He sometimes goes to Paris, though, doesn't he?' she
questioned.

'Occasionally he has to. But he always hurries back.'

'Who wouldn't?' smiled Brooke. 'This is a blissful
spot.'

'You—like it?' A puzzled frown had come to Stephanie's brow.

'Who could help it?' Brooke sighed, and cut into a
piece of meat. 'Jourdain's ancestors must have been very
sensitive people to have built this beautiful château in
such a wonderful . . .'

'You're not thinking of staying, are you?' Stephanie
butted in bluntly, any such idea being quite obviously
more than she could stand.

Brooke swallowed her hurt. Quite plainly, Stephanie
could not wait for her to be gone. She told her calmly, 'I
thought, since I don't start my secretarial course for some
weeks yet, that I might stay on for a while.'

'But you can't!' Stephanie rubbed salt in the wound.

'Of course I can,' Brooke replied blithely. 'Apart from
anything else, I've no wish to offend Jourdain,' she lied—
strangely, without difficulty. 'You heard him say
yourself,' she went on, 'that he'd find it unthinkable I
should stay anywhere except in his home while I'm in
Normandy.'

'But you only came to Normandy because . . .'

'Because of you,' Brooke told her, and grabbed at the
chance while she had it. 'If you want me out of here,
Stephanie, you'll have to come with me.'

'Like hell I will!' Stephanie scorned bad temperedly,
and throwing down her serviette, she slammed from the
room.

If Stephanie had lost her appetite, then so had Brooke.

She had the disturbed feeling, as she laid down her knife
and fork, that she had played it all wrong. Stephanie had
been dreadfully spoiled, she admitted that, but always
before when she displayed uncaring insolence, Brooke
had been able to get through to her. But always before,
her manner of dealing with Stephanie had been to use
gentle understanding persuasion.

Brooke recognised then that her own personality
seemed to have undergone a change since she had come
to the château and met its owner. Aside from the fact that
she had met Stephanie's insolence head on, without any
attempt to coax her out of it, she had lost her usual calm
demeanour a couple of times when, without precedent,
she had fired up at Jourdain Marchais.

Thoughts of him, and of how she was committed to be
part of some 'mutual attraction' farce—when he had
about as much liking for her as she had for him—had her
spirits at a low ebb.

She tried to cheer herself up by thinking of her home in
England. But that only brought the memory of her father,
and how, today of all days, the day of his promotion
interview, she should be at home with him. If his
interview went badly, he would be depressed and would
need to have someone he could talk to.

Pulled two ways, quite unable to be in two places at
once, Brooke owned to being totally and utterly fed up. A
few seconds later, a flash of rebellion took her. As her
eyes lit on the wine carafe, she thought, why not? and
poured herself a glass.

Her mood of rebellion lasted for about as long as it
took her to down the wine—which left her feeling no
better. Yet when she left the table, she was convinced
that something about Jourdain Marchais, or being away
from home, had taken hold of her. For impotent though
her revolt had been, it was new to her personality.

She wandered from the *salle-à-manger*. With the rain still pouring down outside she was uncertain what to do. A walk was out, and she felt no wish to go and find Stephanie only to invite another helping of her rudeness.

In a restless mood, Brooke wandered into the *salon*, took a chair near the window, and gazed out at the pouring rain. How long she sat with her eyes taking in the paths, the gardens, and the small copse beyond, she had no idea. But all at once, in that peaceful setting, her feeling of restlessness ebbed. She closed her eyes to shut out the view, but her unease did not return.

It was most peculiar, she thought, that when her problems seemed to increase by the hour, such small things as the charm of the room, and the view from the window, should be able to work such a spell over her.

She refused to open her eyes when a feeling of drowsiness came over her. Instead she adjusted her position and let her head rest against the back of the chair. She didn't need the distraction of the superb view out there; she needed to think.

Her feeling of drowsiness increased when she found she was chasing around the same thoughts as before. With no fresh enlightenment coming to her, Brooke grew weary of going over the same ground. The way out that Jourdain Marchais had outlined appeared to be the only one with any chance of success.

A picture of him with a devilish light in those amused grey eyes floated before her. Quickly she banished him. He was bad enough in the flesh without her mind's eye conjuring him up! She forced her thoughts away from him, away from Stephanie, and away from France.

She really ought to ring her father tonight to ask how his interview had gone. He would be bound to mention Stephanie, though, if only to ask whether she had seen anything of her yet. Her thoughts had started to run away with her, and Jourdain Marchais was suddenly looming large in any proposed phone call she might make, when Brooke fell asleep.

Something touching her mouth made her open her eyes. Not properly awake, she guessed her sleep must have been sound and deep for it caused her no alarm to see Jourdain Marchais bent over her.

'Did—you—kiss me?' she found herself asking him in a halfhearted, half-asleep fashion.

'Your lips, parted in sleep, were too irresistible,' he replied gravely.

'Oh,' said Brooke, quite stupidly, she thought, and more because she felt she should rather than because she wanted to, she got up from her chair.

Jourdain did not step back to allow her the passage she needed. Her body brushed against his, and in the next moment he had folded her gently into his arms.

'Quite—irresistible,' he murmured, looking down into her sleepy face.

Why she did not push him away or hit him then, Brooke did not know. For the fact that he had it in mind to kiss her again was clearly telegraphed when, his look quizzical, his head started to come down.

In the next moment it was too late for her to do anything. For Jourdain's mouth was over her own and, suddenly, a whole new world was opening up for her. She was not sure, in that first kiss, if she kissed him back or not. All she knew then was that she liked the feel of his warmth, and his manly strength. For years she had put all her endeavours into trying to make her family feel secure, but now, with Jourdain's strong arms about her, she was the one to feel safe for a change. She enjoyed the feeling.

Briefly Jourdain took his mouth from hers and stared down in sea-green eyes that were neither cold nor angry. Gently he kissed her again. As Brooke's arms crept up and around him the pressure of his mouth on hers increased. His arms tightened about her, and Brooke knew more security.

Jourdain's embrace was evoking feelings in her which she could not, and did not wish to deny. But, just when she had begun to respond freely, a heartfelt cry abruptly shattered any illusion of security.

Jerking away from Jourdain, she looked to the door where a white-faced Stephanie stood. Shock and horror were on her young sister's face as she whispered, her eyes on Jourdain, 'I heard your car . . .' It was obvious that Stephanie had stayed only to tidy herself before rushing down to see him. Clearly unable to cope with the scene she had come across she turned and bolted out of sight.

If Brooke had spent some minutes in a dream world, she came fully awake now. Any peace she had imagined in Jourdain's arms vanished without trace. Her intelligence was awakened to the fact that he had deliberately set that scene up, and that it had absolutely nothing to do with him finding her lips 'quite irresistible'.

'You knew full well Stephanie would come looking for you when she heard your car,' she delayed going after her sister to accuse him. 'You left that door open on purpose, because you knew Stephanie would look in! You . . .'

'Suppose I did?' he cut in smoothly, admitting nothing, his eyes on hers. 'Was it not what we agreed—to be enamoured with each other for Stephanie to see?'

'Yes, but . . .' Brooke broke off, and had to look away from him. She realised that she had better keep quiet about her decision not to give Stephanie more than verbal proof that she and Jourdain were interested in each other.

Suddenly Stephanie, her hands up to her face as though brushing away tears, flashed by the window.

Brooke dropped her conversation with Jourdain at

once. Stephanie was hurt, and in tears! Without word or excuse to her host, or with any thought to what she was going to say to Stephanie when she caught up with her, Brooke took off.

The depths of Stephanie's unhappiness bit into Brooke when she ran out into a downpour. Normally, Stephanie would never have risked her blonde curls in such inclement weather.

Following her, Brooke raced past the window of the *salon*. If Jourdain Marchais was looking out and found it amusing that his two English guests should think it fine sport to run about in the pelting rain, she did not wish to know.

Without a glance to the window, she went on along the route Stephanie had taken. At the end of the building, with her sister nowhere to be seen, Brooke turned and went a way she had not been before. The concrete path soon ran out and then became a gravel path. When that ran out, Brooke discovered that the dirt path which took over led down to a tree-lined river walk.

Her mind taken up with catching Stephanie, Brooke had no time in which to admire this fresh beauty. Stephanie must have come this way, she thought. If she had gone the other way, Brooke would have seen her.

Brooke made it to the river path and looking at a left-hand bend she caught a glimpse of the brightly coloured shirt Stephanie was wearing. Still running, she nearly called out to her, but a belief that her sister would either hide or put on a faster turn of speed held her back from crying Stephanie's name.

But a cry was indeed heard. Such a cry of anguish that Brooke stopped dead. The next moment her heart almost stopped dead too. Following that wail that sounded as if Stephanie's pain was too great to bear, Brooke heard a sound that absolutely petrified her. It was the noise of a splash—the splash of someone going into the *river*!

Fear tore at Brooke's heart. 'Oh, dear heaven, no!' she whispered, and sprinted off, Stephanie's words, 'If you do anything to spoil this for me—I'll kill myself!' screaming in her head with every step.

CHAPTER FOUR

BROOKE prayed as she sped along the river path that Stephanie's 'I'll kill myself!' had been pure dramatics and nothing more. But when she rounded the bend, her worst fears were justified: Stephanie was in the water. Brooke wasted no time. The next second she had jumped in to save her.

Only Stephanie did not want to be saved. 'Get away from me!' she screamed when Brooke tried to grab hold of her.

Brooke did not waste her breath in argument and tried another grab for her. Then she saw that, by some great fortune, Stephanie had moved nearer to the bank in her attempt to put some space between them. The water there was about a metre deep, and like a collie rounding up a stray sheep, Brooke waded to the back of her; her ploy working in that Stephanie moved yet closer to the bank.

A movement on that bank took Brooke's eyes away from her, to note that Jourdain was there. It seemed that he had no intention of ruining his clothes by diving in to lend a hand, but he began to speak to Stephanie calmly in French.

What he was saying Brooke had no clue, but whatever it was it had the effect of a small miracle. For although Stephanie was now sobbing hysterically, she waded towards him and allowed him to pull her out of the water.

He was still talking soothingly to her when Brooke made it to the bank. He had no word for her in any language, though. A sardonic lift of his right eyebrow at he waterlogged sight she looked when she dragged herself out of the water was his only acknowledgement of her. He picked Stephanie up in his arms, and, using the short cut he must have come by to have been there at all, he left a distraught Brooke to trail after them.

She was heedless of the rough treatment the luxurious carpets of the château were put to, when, still dripping water, she squelched up the stairs behind Jourdain and his cargo. Her mind was extremely troubled and she was vaguely aware that Jourdain, catching sight of the maid Emilie, had issued some instruction, but that was about all.

Jourdain did not set Stephanie down until he had carried her through her bedroom and into her bathroom. By then the calming words he had spoken to her as they trudged along had quietened her sufficiently for her to make some reply.

What she said, Brooke was unable to understand. She went forward with the intention of getting her out of her sodden clothes, but she could not fail to comprehend Stephanie's scream of, 'You leave me alone!'

Jourdain's rapid French prevented Brooke from saying anything—although what she would have said, she did not know. When Stephanie, although still in tears, quietened again at Jourdain's words, it was all too clear that, while the scene she had witnessed in the *salon* had left her infatuation for him unaffected, it had strengthened her present hatred for her elder sister.

Pride made Brooke try hard to hide her unhappiness, but, as Madame Lasserre came to join them, she guessed Jourdain had seen it. For his tone was kinder than she had heard it, when he suggested quietly, 'Why not go and get into some dry clothes, Brooke. My housekeeper will cope here.'

A quick glance at Stephanie showed she would start

screaming again if Brooke so much as laid a finger on her. So without a word to any of them, she left them to it, her chin tilted a proud fraction higher.

She stayed that way until she had closed the door of her room behind her, then pride and everything else collapsed, like a pricked balloon. Her young sister had just attempted to commit suicide!

Her mind in torment, Brooke threw off her clothes and stepped under a hot shower. Lashed by remorse at her part in the event, Brooke had never been more unhappy in her life.

By the time she had dried off, and was dressed in trousers and a light sweater, anger had started to stir however. Part of that anger was for herself. Forgetting her poor night's sleep, she blamed the glass of wine she had consumed at lunchtime for making her doze in the *salon*. Never, she vowed, would she ever drink wine at lunchtime again—not while she was here anyhow. If she hadn't nodded of, Jourdain Marchais would never have had the chance to come in and kiss her awake. Thoughts of his kisses and how aware of herself he had made her were quickly pushed away; the rest of her anger was reserved for him.

Mingled with that anger was guilt that, for an instant, she had been prepared to so much as *pretend* to go along with him and his scheme to make Stephanie want to go home.

She was still of a mind to take her sister home and the quicker the better. But first Brooke must see her, must see how she was, and, if Stephanie would let her, she must talk to her.

Brooke was unsure, as she opened her door, if she was going to make a clean confession of every word which had passed between her and Jourdain. Then, as she started to leave her room, she almost cannoned into him coming along the landing. Abruptly she halted. He stopped too.

He had changed from the clothes which had come to grief when he had carried her dripping wet sister back to the château, she saw. Thoughts of her sister strayed from Brooke's mind as she looked at the mouth that had kissed her, and her colour deepened. She recognised then, that her nerve ends must be all of a jangle. She had already owned to the discovery of a new person within her since she had known Jourdain Marchais, and at what he had to say, that new person took over once again.

The curve on his mouth had become a smile, she saw, and there was something akin to admiration in his eyes when as he scanned her still damp hair, the only visible sign that she had been waterlogged, he murmured humorously,

'The—er—running jump *you* took, *petite*, has done nothing to impair your beauty.'

Her fury on the upsurge, Brooke ignored his compliment. To learn that he must have seen her jump into the river after her sister was one thing, but that he could refer to it so callously—and even think it *funny*—was more than her jangled nerves could take. She had to hit out. As luck would have it, Jourdain was just near enough for her to score a direct hit.

His look of utter astonishment when her hand flew through the air and connected with a resounding crack took some of the fury from Brooke. That would serve for any reply he might be expecting, she thought with satisfaction. Without a word, she took the few paces to Stephanie's room and went inside. If he was still thunderstruck with astonishment, she was totally unconcerned.

Madame Lasserre was with Stephanie, and Brooke saw she had worked quickly to get her sister cleaned up and into bed. Perhaps bed was the best place for her, she thought, but from the glare of dislike she received as she approached, she knew that her sister had not warmed to her at all.

'How are you, love?' she asked gently.

For answer, Stephanie presented her with her back, and closed her eyes. At which Madame Lasserre, in the split French and English they had adopted, smiled at Brooke, and told her, 'Monsieur instructed the *sédatif*. Mademoiselle Stephanie *a maintenant sommeil*.'

Brooke found a smile for the housekeeper, understanding her to say that a sedative had made Stephanie feel sleepy. Loath though she was to agree with anything Jourdain Marchais had instructed, she had to accept that sleep might be beneficial for Stephanie.

'*Merci, madame,*' she thanked the housekeeper, more for what she had done for Stephanie than for what she had just told her, and with another glance at her sister, she went back to her own room.

The whole situation was worse than a nightmare, she thought. Unable to sit calmly, she paced up and down. The only certainty in her head was that it was more important than ever to get Stephanie back to England.

Thoughts of Stephanie, combined with feelings of guilt, buzzed around and around in her head. Finally she started to have doubts about her wisdom in coming to the château to collect her sister. But how could she have done anything else? Surely it would have been negligent in the extreme just to accept the contents of Stephanie's letter, without any attempt to do something about it?

Consequences of the attempt she had made were so horrifying that Brooke felt barely able to take any more. It wasn't all her fault, she argued, when her guilt became too much for her. She hadn't known Jourdain Marchais was going to kiss her.

She hadn't known either, butted in the voice of her honest conscience, that she would respond to the wretched man the way she had. But Brooke did not want to think about that. When her wandering thoughts remembered the security she had felt in his arms, and the thrill she had experienced at receiving his kisses, Brooke decided enough was enough. She just could not face going around in circles again—this time in an endeavour to understand just what had come over her. It was over, finished with, and the sooner Jourdain Marchais knew it the better. Then she remembered the way she had hit him. Probably he already knew that any make-believe love affair between them was over.

Anger stirred in her again when she recalled the callous humour that had earned him that slap, and a determined light entered her eyes. To have spoken the way he had done only underlined how uncaring he was about Stephanie's attempted suicide.

Well, they did not need him to care. Tomorrow, whatever lies she had to tell, even if she had to tell Stephanie that their father was desperately ill—though she hoped it wouldn't come to that—they were going home.

Thoughts of her father impinged, and she dearly wanted to know the outcome of his interview. To ring him now, though, was out of the question. Upset as she was, she had no faith that she would be able to keep the anxiety she felt out of her voice in any call she made. If her father had been offered promotion, he would be cock-a-hoop. How could she confess the terrible happenings of the day? If his interview had gone badly, how could she add to his depression?

Tomorrow, she decided, would be soon enough to acquaint her father with as little of the facts as she could get away with. Meantime, she would observe one last courtesy to Jourdain Marchais, their host.

Quickly, before she changed her mind at the expense of her deeply imbued good manners, Brooke left her room and went downstairs. She had no idea what kind of sedative Stephanie had swallowed, but she might well not surface in time for dinner. Brooke, with no intention of dining *à deux* with Jourdain, was hopeful that this was the last time she would have to see him.

Her sortie into the *salon* showed no sign of him. But, determined to have her last meeting with him over and done, she went to a door at the far end of the hall. If she had worked out her geography correctly, this should be his study. She tapped lightly, then went in.

It was indeed the study, but Jourdain Marchais, although he was seated behind a huge antique desk, seemed to have been staring into space rather than hard at work.

His movements unhurried, he was on his feet, nevertheless, before Brooke had turned from closing the door. She had been hoping to keep calm throughout this shortest of interviews, but he started her anger vibes throbbing, when mindful of the last time she had seen him, he mocked lightly,

'This is—or should I say, I hope this is—an unexpected pleasure.'

She would not apologise for hitting him. She would not! He had deserved that slap and more. To her mind, he was taking the whole issue much too lightly.

'The pleasure was all mine,' she told him acidly. The curve that came to his mouth told her, infuriatingly, that she had amused him yet again. 'I'll get straight to the point, although it will come as no surprise to you, I'm sure,' she went on hurriedly lest he should butt in with some other mocking remark, 'that since the—the ridiculous notion of our pretending to be smitten with ach other has had such disastrous results for Steph . . .'

'Disastrous?' As she had been afraid he might, he interrupted her before she could come to the end. Yet he seemed genuinely puzzled and at a loss to know why his ridiculous idea had been such a disaster, and Brooke's anger suddenly got out of her control.

'Wouldn't you say,' she challenged furiously, 'that it was disastrous that my sister should try to drown herself?'

'Drown herself?' he echoed, his look so astounded that Brooke was taken aback for a moment.

'What the blazes did you think she was doing in the river in the pouring rain,' she fired, 'if she wasn't attempting to commit suicide?'

Jourdain gave some sort of a grunt, then looked down at his desk. His astonishment had gone, though he looked thoughtful as he raised steady grey eyes to her.

'So—that is why you jumped into the river fully clothed,' he said, as if speaking his thoughts aloud. 'It was not part of your eccentric English nature.' Suddenly his voice had softened, 'You thought Stephanie was trying to drown herself and, very bravely, you jumped in to rescue . . .'

'Stephanie *was* trying to drown herself,' Brooke cut in sharply, wondering just who he thought he was to call her eccentric! 'Because she saw—she saw——' she started to feel uncomfortable, but made herself finish, '. . . me—with you—in the *salon*.'

The smile was back in his eyes. 'Ah, is that why you took a—swipe—at me, because I kissed you in the *salon*?' Hot words rushed to her lips, but before she could speak, his mouth had started to quirk upwards. There was nothing wrong with his memory, when he added, 'Your reaction to my kiss was less—belated, I think.'

Brooke promptly came to the end of her tether. She

erupted furiously, with not a sign of calm about her, 'I hit you because, with my sister so distressed, I found your callous attitude more than I could take. But,' she charged on, determined to go on talking even if he attempted to interrupt, 'you can be as callous as you like from now on. I'm taking Stephanie home tomorrow whether she wants to go or not!' With that she marched to the door, and had one final thing to say when she turned then. 'For myself,' she hurled at him furiously, 'I can't wait to leave!'

An hour later, she had cooled down enough to wonder what it was about Jourdain Marchais that so disturbed her usual tranquil way of dealing with matters. She had been determined to retain her good manners and to tell him, civilly and courteously, that she and Stephanie were leaving. Yet the way she had exploded and had slammed out of his study had nothing tranquil about it.

Having had her fill of self-examination, Brooke wanted no more, and she gave in to the urge she had been suppressing to go and see if Stephanie was awake. Silently she went to her sister's room, ready to tiptoe out again if she was still asleep. Carefully she turned the door handle and popped her head around the door.

'What do you want?' was the greeting she got for her pains. Stephanie, looking none the worse for her wetting, was sitting up in bed reading a magazine, clearly at her most belligerent.

'How are you feeling?' Brooke asked quietly, and advanced into the room.

'How do you think I'm feeling? How would any girl feel to find out her sister is making out with her man behind her back?'

Brooke almost told her everything then. The words were all there to tell her how she had been ready to go along with Jourdain's suggestion of a pretended attraction between them, so long as it was kept to words, not actions. She even got as far as, 'Stephanie love . . .' when the memory flooded back, of the active way she had responded to him when he had held her in his arms, and what she had been about to say stayed stuck in her throat. There had been nothing of pretence in her response to him, and she could not say otherwise.

'Yes, Brooke dear?' Stephanie mimicked. 'Were you about to try to tell me that what I saw was conceived solely in my imagination? That I didn't see . . .'

'No,' Brooke butted in. She realised that seeing her locked in an embrace with Jourdain had not, as he had suggested, had the effect of making Stephanie, with her pride uppermost, want to go home. Perhaps there might be another way. 'You saw what you saw,' she agreed. 'I'd nodded off in the *salon*, and when Jourdain came in, he kissed me, but it meant nothing to him. Don't you understand the type of man he is, love?' she went on urgently. 'He'll kiss when he can, and he just isn't interested in taking any girl seriously.'

'I never thought he was a saint,' Stephanie snapped petulantly. 'But if you're trying to tell me he doesn't care for me, you can forget it, because I know he does!' She went on, as if bringing out an ace, 'Why, only five minutes ago he sent Madame Lasserre to tell me I mustn't think of getting up for dinner. That I must rest for the remainder of the day, and that dinner will be brought to my room. If that's not caring for me, you tell me what is!'

Brooke could have told her that Jourdain's concern had only come about since she had shaken him by revealing that they were not a pair of English eccentrics, but that Stephanie had in fact attempted to drown herself. But she did not. She had no wish to remind Stephanie of her suicide attempt. Once they were home in England she would get her to talk it all out of her system. For the moment she must concentrate on getting her sister on a more even keel. So all she said was a light,

'Who could know you, and not—like—you, Stephanie?'

'Soft soap?' Stephanie queried truculently.

Brooke smiled. 'What I should have said,' she amended, 'was who could know you when you forget to be a crosspatch, and not like you. Now,' she said briskly, 'if you're to have dinner in bed, I'd better straighten you up. 'Your bedcover is all over the . . .'

'I'm not having dinner in bed!'

'But you've just said . . .'

'If you think I'm staying stuck up here while you make all the headway you can with Jourdain over a cosy dinner for two, you can think again!' Stephanie told her in no uncertain terms.

'Headway—with that man!' exclaimed Brooke. 'Good grief, Stephanie, I don't even *like* him!'

'What a quaint way you have of showing it,' came the jibe.

Brooke rather thought she had asked for that one, and could only reply, 'Believe me, love, I've no wish to see Jourdain Marchais ever again. I'd already decided not to go down to dinner tonight.'

Stephanie stared at her as if trying to discern the truth. 'Good,' she said, and then to let her know she had nothing more she wanted to add, she snuggled down in the covers and closed her eyes.

Brooke hesitated, but in her heart of hearts she knew that this was just not the right moment to tell Stephanie they were going home the next day. She decided to come back later, and stayed only long enough to tuck the covers more snugly around her. Then she went back to her own room to try to dream up some way to ensure that Stephanie would be with her on that ferry tomorrow.

She had still not thought up anything which did not involve telling a direct lie, when there was a tap on her door. Much to her surprise she saw Emilie standing there holding a dinner tray.

'Oh, this must be for Stephanie.' Too quickly she assumed that Emilie had come to the wrong door.

'*Non, mademoiselle,*' said Emilie when Brooke tried to redirect her, and with a babble of French she moved into the room and set her burden down. She was still chattering away when she went out, the smile she offered as she went off showing that she had no objection to bringing the meal up the stairs to Brooke.

Brooke objected, though. It was because she did not want anyone to fetch and carry for her that she had told no one other than Stephanie that she would not be going down to dinner. It had been her opinion that she could cope with any pangs of hunger which came from a missed meal.

She took the cover from the tray and, rather than send it back to the kitchen untouched, began to eat, her thoughts on how her ear for the French language had improved during her short stay. For, although most of what Emilie had rattled off had been incomprehensible, somehow it had come across that Mademoiselle Stephanie had said her sister would not be down to dinner either, whereupon the master had instructed that a second tray should be sent upstairs.

Torn between guilt, that the staff should have to put themselves out for her able-bodied self, and self-congratulation that her ear was becoming attuned to the language, Brooke finished her meal. Given time and a lot of effort, she could, if she wanted, be as fluent in that language as everyone else, she decided.

But time in France was something she did not have. Why she should feel a pang at that thought, she could not have said. It was so totally ridiculous. Why, she couldn't wait for tomorrow so that she could get away.

That thought motivated her into getting out her suitcase to start to pack. This time tomorrow, she *and* Stephanie would be back in their own beds.

Her packing completed apart from the last-minute items, it then occurred to Brooke that, since Stephanie had been at the château for so much longer, all the things she had brought with her, added to those she had no doubt purchased since, would take far longer to pack.

She glanced at her watch and saw that it had gone nine. She could delay no more in going to see her sister. She was aware that she would have to tread carefully in the conversation which was to take place, but she was still determined to tell whatever lie she had to in order to get the result she wanted.

Brooke opened her door and was halfway between the two rooms when the sound of girlish laughter stopped her dead. She would know the sound of Stephanie laughing and in happy spirits anywhere. As well as she would know the baritone laugh that had just joined in.

A dart of pain speared her, and she moved without knowing she had done so. She came to, to find she had turned about, hurried back to her room, and had quietly closed the door.

She felt quite ill suddenly, and went to sit on her bed. Nothing if not honest, Brooke had to face the fact that Stephanie, with not a scrap of hysteria in her laughter, had been sharing some joke with Jourdain Marchais. And she, Brooke, had not liked it.

That honest admission caused Brooke not a little confusion. For when she tried to find out why she had not liked it, the word 'jealousy' separated itself from all others.

Oh, goodness, she thought in self-disgust, and then

knew more confusion. Fearful that she had become
something she did not want to be—a possessive sister—
she went on to analyse her feelings, and found that she
could not be sure if she had been jealous of Stephanie
laughing with Jourdain—or of Jourdain laughing with
Stephanie!

Whatever the facts, Brooke could not bring herself to
open her door again that night to investigate that last
idea further. She went to bed and planned that, if they
caught the afternoon ferry, there would be the whole
morning in which to pack Stephanie's belongings, and let
her say her goodbyes. She went to sleep, but did not sleep
well. Yet in her wakeful moments there was no room in
her head to remember that the best laid plans . . .'

She was up and about early, not at all impressed that
on this, the day she was going home, the sky was blue and
it looked as if the sun would shine the whole day through,
for a change.

She bathed and dressed in the cotton slacks and shirt
in which she was going to travel home, and packed the
last of her possessions. She checked her watch, and
certain that Stephanie must be either awake or stirring,
braced herself and went along the landing.

She opened the door to her sister's room, and entered.
It was then that all Brooke's plans fell apart. For
although Stephanie was wide awake and sitting up in
bed, Brooke only had to hear her laboured breathing to
know that her sister was not going anywhere that day.
Stephanie needed a doctor, not a ferry trip. Brooke had
nursed her through too many asthma attacks not to know
that she was in need of medical help. And without that
help, her dear sister could be seriously ill!

CHAPTER FIVE

BROOKE went swiftly to the bed, trying hard to keep the lid down on her panic. Stephanie's laboured breathing foretold that she might start wheezing at any moment.

'You're a fine one,' she said calmly, no need for her to ask unnecessary questions which her sister did not seem to have the breath to answer anyway. 'Hold on, darling,' she bade her, and turned back to her own room to grab the pillows from her bed.

In no time she was back and was padding up the pillows behind Stephanie. 'Sit forward, chick,' she instructed, 'and do your best to relax.'

'My—chest—hurts,' Stephanie laboured to complain.

'I know it does,' Brooke tried to soothe her. 'But we'll soon have that put right. Just sit tight. I'll be back in two shakes,' she urged, as she walked to the door.

Outside the room, Brooke went into action her feet flying down the stairs. Instinct, maybe from yesterday's knowledge of how Jourdain breakfasted early, made her go straight to the breakfast room.

'I need a doctor,' she addressed the French newspaper held up in front of her host.

'A doctor!' The paper was lowered, a look of genuine concern in Jourdain's face as he got rapidly to his feet. 'You are ill, Brooke?'

'No, not me,' she told him impatiently. 'It's Stephanie.'

'She was well enough last night,' Jourdain wasted time telling her what she already knew. Brooke was more than well aware of how the pair of them had been laughing at

86

some shared joke.

'Well, she isn't well now,' she told him, starting to panic again. 'She's going into an asthma attack, and needs medical attention straight away.'

'Stephanie's an asthmatic?' he queried, this information obviously news to him.

If he was going to take exception to the fact that no one had thought to forewarn him of this when he had agreed to take Stephanie into his home, Brooke had no time to listen. She had no time either to give him a rundown on her sister's medical history.

'She isn't any more. Or she wasn't,' she told him worriedly. 'But she's in trouble now. Will you please call a . . .' She had no need to say more. As Jourdain's eyes rested on the agitation in her eyes, he took charge.

'Go to her,' he commanded. 'A doctor will be here very shortly.'

It was all she waited to hear. She was off, back up the stairs. Outside Stephanie's room, she paused. A second later she had recaptured some semblance of calm, and went in.

She had not expected to see any improvement in Stephanie and there was none. 'The doctor will be here soon,' she told her sister, hoping that would comfort her a little.

For a moment, as Stephanie gasped, 'A—doctor,' Brooke had the oddest impression that her sister was appalled at the idea. Then she remembered—Stephanie had an awful dread of going into hospital.

'It's all right, love,' she soothed quietly, 'we've caught this one well in time. You won't be going anywhere near a hospital.'

When Stephanie would have answered, Brooke patted her hand and told her not to try to speak. Praying that she was right and that Stephanie would not get worse before the doctor arrived, Brooke was still talking soothingly to her, when Jourdain arrived with Madame Lasserre in his wake.

Brooke's attention was distracted for perhaps a minute when Madame Lasserre, noting the extra pillows, engaged her in brief conversation, from which she gathered that more pillows for Stephanie and her own bed would shortly be forthcoming. Brooke turned her attention back to the bed to see that Stephanie had managed to find a brave smile in response to whatever expression of sympathy Jourdain must have extended.

Activity was the watchword after that. Madame Lasserre went out, coming back with more pillows, and in no time the doctor had arrived, and she was showing him up the stairs.

'Ah, Matthieu,' said Jourdain, and as Madame Lasserre departed, he went to shake hands with the fair-haired man who appeared to be about the same age as himself. Jourdain turned to Brooke, 'Permit me to introduce my friend of some years, Dr Matthieu Delage. Miss Brooke Farringdon,' he completed the formalities in English, 'who is honouring us with a visit from England.'

Brooke had only the briefest moment in which to think 'honouring!', then the doctor, his eyes on her fine complexion, had warmly taken hold of her hand. His eyes were showing warmth too when, clearly liking what he saw, he murmured, *'Enchanté, mademoiselle . . .'* Then Jourdain, as if he did *not* like what *he* saw, cut in tersely to state,

'Your patient, my friend, is here.'

Jourdain stayed only long enough to introduce Stephanie. Then, without a glance at Brooke, he left them to it.

No sooner had the door closed than, completely

professional, the doctor concentrated his skills on Stephanie. Brooke stood by while he checked her sister's pulse, then tapped at her chest. Fear gnawed away at her when, at the sound that echoed back, Brooke saw the doctor quickly mask a look of disconcertion.

He was a good doctor, she realised quickly, for he then proceeded to put Stephanie through a very thorough examination. He had an excellent bedside manner too, and now and then he would throw in some casual comment which suggested his attention was off Stephanie, but which gave him more chance to watch her unobserved.

By the end of his examination Brooke had learned that he was quite conversant in her language, and he in turn knew that, while Stephanie could speak his country's language, her sister could not.

Which made Brooke sure that he meant no discourtesy, and that it must have been a slip of the tongue, when, as he put his stethoscope away, he addressed Stephanie in a stream of French. Stephanie, her French not so fast because of her breathlessness replied in kind and Brooke was forced to rethink her previous opinion that her ear for the language was improving, for she understood not a word.

What she did understand, though, was that the doctor's questions were not making Stephanie feel any better. She really seemed to be struggling the more his questioning went on. Brooke's love for her sister started to overcome her logic, and she had to hold down hard on the urge to interrupt and tell him he was causing Stephanie distress.

Which was why it came as a shock when, with the words on the tip of her tongue, Dr Delage turned and told her, albeit gently,

'Perhaps you would like to leave us, *mademoiselle*.

Your presence here,' he smiled kindly as if to take the sting from his words, 'appears to cause your sister more distress.'

Her mouth opened to form a surprised 'Oh', and Brooke looked to where Stephanie, in spite of being ill, showed every sign of not liking her.

'I'll wait for your report in in—the *salon*,' she told him, and went quickly from the room.

Still embarrassed at being sent from the room when all she wanted to do was help, Brooke went into the *salon*. Jordain Marchais was far from her thoughts. She was reminded of him, however, when his tall length left the chair he had been occupying in that room.

'Matthieu has finished his examination?' he enquired.

Brooke shook her head, wishing him at work in his study where he should be. Confession, she found, was *not* good for the soul. 'My presence was distressing Stephanie,' she told him honestly.

'You distress *her*?' he queried. 'But how? You have done so much for her, *n'est-ce pas*?

'Oh yes,' snapped Brooke, 'just look what I've done for her! If it hadn't been for yesterday,' she flared, her mind on the scene her sister had witnessed in this very room, 'she wouldn't be in the state she's in now!'

Brooke admitted she was feeling a little frayed around the edges. The instant the words were said, however, she wondered what it was about this man that rattled her equilibrium so often. She half expected him to stand up, but he did nothing of the kind, and with a steady look at her asked mildly,

'You believe the—ducking—Stephanie experienced yesterday is responsible for this attack of asthma?'

The effect of his mild tone, even if he was on the wrong track, made Brooke feel slightly ashamed of her outburst. But, able to quote reams to him on asthma and its causes, she confined herself to telling him,

'Most probably, her—emotional upset of yesterday—her hysteria, has more to do with it. She hasn't had an attack for three years.'

'Which argues that she has been emotionally well adjusted, these last three years,' Jourdain replied, not prepared, she saw, to take on himself any of the blame for the events of yesterday.

'Well, yes, I suppose she has been,' she had to reply.

'Was it emotion that triggered off her first attack?'

'Her first attack occurred shortly after our mother died,' she told him.

'Which was the time when your father went emotionally to pieces?'

'That's perfectly understandable, surely,' Brooke replied defensively, not without a touch of aggression.

'Perfectly,' Jourdain agreed, disarmingly, and smiled gently.

'My father had got himself back together again by the time Stephanie had—what I thought was her last attack,' Brooke muttered. She was left floundering, and wondering again how much of their family life Stephanie had told him, when Jourdain came back,

'Which was about the time your brother, Stephanie's twin, began to be emotionally at odds with the world.'

'He—went through—a phase,' Brooke admitted grudgingly. 'But all youngsters go through a bad patch at that age. Steven is as well adjusted as any of his friends,' she defended him sharply.

'With your patience and help, I believe,' Jourdain put in. Then before she could reply, he went on to send any answer she might have thought of straight from her head. 'How about you, Brooke?' he enquired.

'Me?' she asked, unable to see what he was getting at.

'How about you and your—emotional upsets? Who

helps you when you go through a—bad patch?'

'My emotional upsets!' she exclaimed scornfully. 'Who can afford such luxuries? Who . . .' her voice faded. 'That sounds hard, cynical,' she back-pedalled. 'I didn't mean . . .'

'You're not hard,' Jourdain told her softly. 'You are just so concerned with the other members of your family that you have spared no time to think of yourself.' Brooke blinked, as much from his softer tone as from the fact that this well-to-do, sophisticated man was telling her such things. 'But your emotions should not be suppressed, little one,' he went on. 'I . . .' The sound of the door opening caused him to break off.

Matthieu Delage came in, and Brooke rapidly regained her senses. Only then did she realise how much Jourdain Marchais had softened her mood. Despite his previous reluctance to take her to his bed—if he had to—Jourdain Marchais, ever the flirt, could have just been about to intimate a willingness to go to work on her suppressed emotions!

Abruptly, she forgot him and addressed the doctor. 'Stephanie? What . . .?'

'You have nothing at all to worry about, *mademoiselle*,' Matthieu Delage said quickly, his smile warm as his hand came to touch her shoulder reassuringly. 'In no time your sister will be well again.'

About to ask a relevant question or two, Brooke never got the words out. For just then Jourdain, his soft tone soon gone, cut in and fired a volley of hard-eyed questions in French at the man who belatedly removed his comforting hand from her shoulder.

The doctor replied in his own language. His smile there again for Brooke, he turned to her to translate, 'I have just told Jourdain that I have administered

medication which will ease your sister. Now, *mademoiselle*,' he smiled, 'I have a few instructions for the care of
. .'

'Mademoiselle Farringdon nursed her sister through three years of illness,' Jourdain broke in sharply, appearing to know that for a fact without anyone having told him. But to Brooke's mind, his tone sounded as if he was none too pleased to have illness in his home, and her pride rocketed.

She vowed then that no one at the château was going to be put to any trouble on behalf of Stephanie or herself. She ignored Jourdain Marchais, but found a smile for Matthieu, when she asked him,

'What instructions do you have for me, doctor?'

'Matthieu, please,' he invited. 'As Jourdain told you, I have been his friend, and a friend of his family, for years. I may call you Brooke?' he asked.

She supposed it must be her week for meeting every French flirt in Normandy, but when she caught the glower that came from the other flirt in the *salon*, her pride went up another notch. It was plain he didn't care to have such freedoms taken when she was no family connection whatsoever.

'Of course,' she gave the doctor permission to use her first name, and pride made her add, 'Matthieu.'

The doctor sent her a delighted grin, then took a glance to his watch. 'I am overdue for my office,' he told her with a touch to her arm. 'If you will walk to my car with me, Brooke, I can give you instructions as we go.'

'Mademoiselle needs no instruction,' Jourdain told his friend, as Brooke walked with him toward the door.

'Not three years ago, certainly, Jourdain,' Matthieu agreed as he opened the door for her to go through. 'But medicine and techniques have greatly improved since her sister's last attack.'

The instructions Matthieu Delage gave Brooke on the way to his car had nothing new to them. She was burning to tell him of Stephanie's attempt to kill herself. But somehow it all seemed very melodramatic now that she had come to terms with the shock of it. Besides, even if the doctor ought to know everything there was to know, it seemed a betrayal of Stephanie to tell him.

'Make sure she keeps up with the tablets I left her, and that she has plenty of fluids,' Matthieu Delage instructed as he got into his car. 'Your sister is relaxed now from the medication I gave her, and I will call again in the morning. But, Brooke,' he smiled from the car's open window, 'do not hesitate to call me if you are in the least worried.'

She thanked him, then went back inside the château and straight up to her sister's room. Miraculously, she saw that the medication Stephanie had swallowed had worked wonders. Faintly amazed, and cheered that in such a relatively short time as three years such progress had been made in medicine to counter an asthma attack, Brooke went to stand close to the bed.

But she was soon to discover that, if Stephanie was no longer struggling to release each exhaled breath, her mood towards Brooke had not evened out.

'You sound better,' Brooke remarked cheerfully.

'I don't feel better,' her sister replied grumpily.

'You soon will.' Brooke retained her cheerful exterior. 'Are these the tablets Dr Delage left you?' she asked, taking up the phial from the bedside table to examine them. The tablets were not at all familiar, but, since they must be new on the market, she had hardly expected to recognise them. 'Can you manage a little something light to eat?' she pressed on when all that came from the bed was a stubborn silence.

'I want nothing,' Stephanie replied, which did not

isturb Brooke too much since her sister's appetite had
lways disappeared when she had an attack—little and
ften, had been the order of the day then. What did
isturb her, though, when always before in panic
tephanie had never been able to bear to let Brooke out
f her sight, was that she should erupt suddenly, 'I want
o be alone!'

'All right, Greta Garbo,' Brooke teased, 'I'll leave you
o rest.' Her teasing brought no response. Stephanie did
how some semblance of the sweeter person she knew her
o be, though, when, reluctantly, and with just a trace of
pology, she volunteered,

'Dr Delage said I must rest all I could.'

'Of course you must,' Brooke agreed gently. 'The
octor is calling again in the morning. If you rest all
oday, then perhaps he'll let you sit out of bed tomorrow.'

She was already considering that, what with this new
nedication and everything, there seemed every chance
f taking Stephanie home if not tomorrow, then possibly
ne day after. Then, to put the lid on all such thoughts,
tephanie told her,

'Dr Delage has insisted I stay in bed for a whole week.'

'A whole week!' Brooke exclaimed, but even as she
vondered if Stephanie's attack was even worse than she
ad thought, she strove for calm. 'Well, a week in bed
ever hurt anyone,' she smiled.

Her efforts to stay calm, as well as her smile, were
vasted, she saw. For Stephanie, looking so relaxed it
vasn't true, had closed her eyes, and showed every
ppearance of wanting to go to sleep. Without saying
nother word Brooke left the room.

In her own room she fretted for some while about the
egree of seriousness of Stephanie's attack. Perhaps this
ew medication had side-effects which might necessitate
ed-rest even when the attack was over. Her thoughts

sped on to wonder if Stephanie would again be struggling
with her breathing once the effect of the medication had
worn off.

At the end of her cogitations, Brooke realised that all
she could do was to wait and see.

Oh grief, she thought, when those words 'wait and see'
repeated themselves in her brain. Less than twenty-four
hours ago she had told Jourdain Marchais that she and
Stephanie were going home today. Not only that, she had
also flung at him, before she had slammed out of his
study, 'For myself, I can't wait to leave!'

Her pride was in ashes as she saw that she was going to
have to seek him out and eat one enormous slice of
humble pie. It was too late then to wish she had not been
quite so rude to him. For, with Stephanie confined to her
bed for a whole week, she was just going to have to tell
him that she was not leaving, and wanted to stay.

It would have been, oh, so easy, to give in to that voice
which urged that Jourdain would know without her
having to tell him. With Stephanie bed-bound, naturally
she would not leave her. But, kick as she might against
having to ask if she could stay on, Brooke knew that, as a
guest, she owed it to him to tell him what was going on.
For all she knew, that spate of French exchanged with
Matthieu Delage in the *salon* might not have included the
information that Stephanie must stay in bed for a week.
Oh dear, Brooke thought, Jourdain Marchais could well
be waiting, right at this minute, for her to tell him what
was happening.

In the hope that her aggravating host would let her get
her piece said courteously, without making some
comment which would see this interview end with the
same fury as her interview with him yesterday, Brooke
gathered up her self-control and went in search of him.

Her first port of call, his study, yielded no sign of him.

But her cowardly half hope that he had gone out, so that she would be able to delay having to see him, was not gratified. For when she took a glance inside the *salon*, he was still there. The very fact that he did not appear to have moved since she had left the *salon* to walk with Matthieu Delage to his car, only seemed to underline the fact that her host had been waiting for her to show the good manners to enlighten him as to what was going on in his home. The lofty look he favoured her with as she went in seemed to definitely confirm it.

'I'm sorry I've been so long,' she found herself apologising when she wasn't sorry at all, hating herself, and him. 'But I wanted to—er—settle Stephanie first.' The aloof look he gave her from beneath his arrogant brow, plus the fact that he left her to struggle on, sent her hatred of him up another hundred per cent. 'Matthieu said that Stephanie . . .' she began as a lead-up to tell him she had changed her mind about leaving. Jourdain's right eyebrow ascending an arrogant fraction made her falter and try to lead up to it another way. 'He said,' she picked up, 'that he would call again tomorrow.' But Brooke knew, when Jourdain received that information with a dark frown, that nothing she said was going to be right.

'Surely that is not necessary,' he clipped, and while she bit back the words which would have challenged his medical knowledge, he suggested, his tone icily disagreeable, 'but perhaps it is not the younger Miss Farringdon he is calling to see.'

His remark took her breath away. In the next moment, before she could bite back the words, Brooke found she had snapped hotly, 'Don't be ridiculous!'

Arrogance was not the word for the superior way his nostrils flared. All too plainly, no one had ever dared to call him ridiculous before; just as plainly he did not like it.

'Ridiculous!' he snarled. 'You think his only interest lies with your sister's health?' In a tone more than abrasive, he challenged, 'You cannot see—when a man is attracted to you?'

'I'm aware that it comes naturally to a Frenchman to flirt, *monsieur*,' she replied coldly, irked that he should imply that she was so naïve where men were concerned that she couldn't recognise a flirt when she met one. 'Like that of the English eccentric,' she could not resist the jibe, 'the reputation of the French flirt precedes you.'

'*Touché!*' he retorted, uncaring that she had got one back at him. His voice was silky, though, when he added, 'Might I suggest, *mademoiselle*, since we both know you have little experience of your own countrymen, let alone mine, that you check your facts.'

Unsure what he meant, Brooke was stuck to know how to answer. Was he refuting the reputation of his countrymen? Or was he saying that, with her lack of experience, it was doubtful she could tell flirtation from genuine attraction?

'Yes—well,' she said, still in the dark, and not prepared to admit it, with other more important things on her mind, 'we're rather getting away from the point. I didn't come to see you to—er—to have this sort of discussion.'

His arrogant look and the way he looked at her silently as if to say that he would let her know when the point they were discussing was done, made her aware that she had somehow offended him yet again.

She pressed on, pride over what she had to ask making her want to walk from the *salon* and out to her car and drive off. 'The point is that—that Stephanie has been ordered a week's bedrest.' Jourdain showed no surprise, but merely nodded, and Brooke wanted to hit him. She tried hard to stay calm, then forced out, 'I—know I was very rude to you yesterday—when I said I couldn't wait to leave here, 'she went on, the nearest her pride would let her get to an apology, 'but if it's all right with you, I should like to stay on to look after my sister.'

She hated his arrogance, his lofty look, and the fact that he had heard her out without saying one helpful word. She considered he might have unbent more than he did, too, when with the aloof look still on him, he told her stiffly,

'Naturally, you will stay with her.'

'Thank you,' she murmured, but her wretched pride pushed her to tell him, a shade aloofly herself, 'I don't want to inconvenience anyone, and since looking after Stephanie won't take all my time, I can give Madame Lasserre a hand with any . . .'

'I pay staff to do the domestic work,' he chopped her off abruptly, and seemed to be more angered by her offer than anything else, when he told her bluntly, 'you will be better employed, Mademoiselle Farringdon, in putting *all* your energies into getting your sister well again as quickly as possible.'

On that sour note Brooke went swiftly from the *salon.* The man was impossible; as prickly as a hedgehog! Why he should be offended that she should offer to help Madame Lasserre, she didn't know. What she did realise, however, was that from his remark about getting Stephanie well as quickly as possible, Jourdain Marchais couldn't wait to get rid of the pair of them. She'd like to bet that, regardless of his written promise to her father, once Matthieu Delage had declared Stephanie fit to travel, he would forget to be obstructive and would give her all the help he could.

Inwardly fuming, without knowing quite why, because Jourdain's assistance was what she had wanted from the beginning, Brooke went along the hall in search of Madame Lasserre.

She found her in a kitchen that was about four times the size of her kitchen at home, and at the smile of greeting the housekeeper had for her, Brooke's inner anger evaporated.

She would have explained her errand straight away, but Madame Lasserre, expressing concern that she had not yet eaten breakfast, was all ready to have Grace attend on her in the breakfast room. Brooke stopped her, and, at ease with the housekeeper, suggested perhaps they could both have a cup of coffee in the kitchen while she explained a few facts about Stephanie's illness.

Over coffee, in the half French, half English way in which they conversed, Brooke explained that eating a large meal tended to make Stephanie's breathlessness worse. From there, drawing on all her tact, Brooke told the housekeeper that, for a while, Stephanie must eat little and often. Since her sister's appetite had disappeared altogether, she asked if Madame Lasserre would permit her to prepare the things which she knew Stephanie would like most.

'*Mais oui.* Of course,' Madame Lasserre beamed, when Brooke had finished, and added that Grace or Emilie would carry the trays upstairs for her.

'*Non, madame, merci,*' Brooke smiled, 'I carry.' Her coffee finished, she busied herself making Stephanie a small portion of scrambled egg with dainty toast.

From then on, Brooke was barely off her feet. The tablets Matthieu Delage had left were still working wonders in that they kept Stephanie's breathlessness to a minimum, but the changes of mood she went through that day were something about which the medicine could do nothing. Brooke had known in advance that her sister was a terrible patient, although she had forgotton how irritable Stephanie could be during a bout of illness.

At lunchtime she had swung from demanding that Brooke should leave her alone to insisting that she ate her meals nowhere but with her. Since this suited Brooke quite well, she had no objection to going down the stairs again and communicating to Madame Lasserre that she would take her meals with Stephanie, insisting that she could carry her own tray up.

Brooke had her dinner in Stephanie's room too. When she eventually settled her for the night and went to her own room, she admitted to herself that she felt emotionally and physically worn out.

Fresh pillows had been placed in position on her bed at some time during the day, and, feeling tired enough to sleep the clock round, Brooke did not hang about. In no time she was washed and into her nightdress. Only to find that no sooner did she put her head on her pillows than she was wide awake again.

She calculated that anxiety was at the back of her sleeplessness, when a couple of hours had passed with no sign of a visit from the Sandman. Anxiety over Stephanie, of course. She had clapped neither eyes nor ears on Jourdain since she had walked out of the *salon* that morning, but she knew perfectly well that her anxiety had nothing to do with him. It would please her quite well if she never saw or heard him again.

At one o'clock, still wakeful, but aware that the early hours used to be a bad time for Stephanie, she got out of bed and tiptoed along to her room.

Her ears attuned for her sister's breathing, Brooke left Stephanie's door ajar and tiptoed back to her own room. Remarkably, her sister's breathing in sleep was even, and as normal as she had ever heard it.

At three o'clock, the worst time for Stephanie, Brooke was out of bed again, and once more silently skimming along to her sister's room. As before, the only sound to be heard was a natural even sound of someone in a deep and contented sleep.

Brooke backed out of the room, then heard a sound which came from some way up the landing. Startled, she looked up, and was conscious all at once that she had not thought to put on a robe.

'Is everything all right?' Jourdain, his feet and legs bare beneath the robe he had on, came nearer to ask quietly.

'I didn't mean to disturb anyone,' she whispered back guiltily. 'I was just checking on Stephanie, but she's doing well.'

By that time Jourdain was standing straight in front of her, and, suddenly aware of his eyes on her hair, mussed up by the pillow, Brooke felt quite defenceless standing there in her cotton nightdress. Then he smiled and was neither arrogant nor aloof.

'Go back to bed, sweet Brooke,' he murmured, and so saying, he laid a gentle kiss on her cheek. 'Worry no more,' he instructed her as he straightened. 'I'm a light sleeper. I'll keep my door open and listen for Stephanie.'

Feeling slightly mesmerised, although she guessed it was more from tiredness than anything, Brooke did a quick about turn, and did as he had bidden.

A minute after getting into bed, with a hand on the cheek Jourdain had kissed, she went out like a light. She had no idea that she had fallen asleep with a smile on her face.

CHAPTER SIX

A TAP on her door roused Brooke from her sleep the next morning. 'What time is it?' she asked as Grace came into her room, not enough awake to remember the maid did not speak English.

Grace offered her a cheerful, *'Bonjour, mademoiselle,'* and as Brooke sat up, she placed a breakfast tray over her knees.

When she reached for her watch she was staggered to see it had gone eight. Brooke awoke fully. It was a glorious, sunny morning, she had slept like a log, and she was being served breakfast in bed!

'Er—good m ... *Bonjour*, Grace.' She got herself together, but was not up to trying to get through to the maid that she did not want breakfast in bed. *'Merci,'* she thanked her instead.

The maid's reply as she departed was lost on Brooke, for wonderment took hold of her as she removed the cover from the tray and saw that her breakfast consisted of the oh, so English bacon and egg!

A smile at someone's thougthfulness teased her mouth. Suddenly she was starving. Had Madame Lasserre thought of giving her this little treat, she pondered, as she picked up her knife and fork? Or had Jourdain ordered it specially for her? She then recalled his manner with her in the early hours, and touched a hand to her cheek as she remembered his gentle kiss. A feeling of warmth for him started inside her, and somehow she just knew that he was responsible for her English breakfast in bed. Although why he had gone out of his way to be nice to her, was something she could not fathom.

That warm feeling was still there when, having eaten her breakfast, she went to bathe. She had just finished dressing when an explanation for his 'kindness' hit her full-square, and any feeling of warmth promptly disappeared. It was not beyond the realms of possibility, she saw, for Jourdain to have heard about her frequent trips up and down the stairs for Stephanie yesterday. Since he did not want to be saddled with her for longer than he had to, seeing that she consumed a hearty breakfast to energise her day was his way of making sure she did not collapse from lack of nourishment.

She was in a sober frame of mind when she went into her sister's room, and knew what sort of a day she had in front of her when, before she could open her mouth, Stephanie asked complainingly,

'Where have you been?'

'I overslept,' Brooke said calmly. Stephanie's sulky look, however, made her relent. 'I'm sorry you've had to wait for breakfast,' she apologised with a coaxing smile. 'I'll just pop down . . .'

'I've had breakfast. Grace cleared my tray away ages ago,' Stephanie informed her. Brooke determined not to ask if she too had received bacon and egg. 'I'm bored,' her sister moaned.

'Which means,' said Brooke brightly, 'that you must be getting better.'

Stephanie was a pain when she was bored. But Brooke smiled calmly when she went on, 'I feel like hell,' saw to her ablutions, re-made her bed, and gave her a tablet. After which she chased downstairs to find the library, and brought back several books—none of which pleased her sister.

In between trips to the kitchen for the liquid refreshment Stephanie needed, and a visit to make her a light snack round about eleven, Brooke stayed with her sister. It was nearing midday when Grace showed Matthieu Delage into Stephanie's room. Brooke had no wish to be turfed out today as she had been yesterday and waited only to hear Stephanie speak to him in French, before going to wait for him downstairs.

She had been waiting for him in the *salon* for only a few minutes when he came looking for her. The smile he wore told her he held no serious concern for his patient, and this agreed with her own observations. So she was not surprised when, in answer to her questions of how he had found Stephanie, he replied,

'She will soon be up and about.'

'How soon, doctor?' she asked.

'Doctor?' he queried, his look reproving. 'I thought we were friends, Brooke.'

'Matthieu,' she amended, and the question of whether, in his view, Stephanie still needed a whole week in bed was somehow lost, when he said, smiling again,

'That is better. Now to important matters. Am I taking you out to dinner this evening?'

Taken aback for a moment, at this get-in-fast technique, Brooke hurriedly collected herself. 'I'm—er— sorry Matthieu,' she told him politely, 'but Stephanie wishes me to take all my meals with her, and I don't . . .'

'But she is not so ill . . .' the doctor started to argue persuasively, when another voice cut in.

'As I told you, Matthieu, Mademoiselle Farringdon is devoted to her sister,' said Jourdain coolly as he came through the open doorway.

'I understand that, of course,' Matthieu replied. 'But there is no . . .'

'Then you will not try to dissuade her against the dictates of that devotion.' Jourdain cut him off again.

'Neither of you would enjoy a meal under such circumstances.'

Pride niggled away at Brooke and won. She might be a little over-sensitive, but it seemed to her that Jourdain was dead set against the idea of Matthieu Delage taking her anywhere. Well, he needn't worry that she might assume herself a family friend too, for she had no intention of dining with his flirtatious fellow-country-man anyway. She decided she had no part to play in this conversation and—ignoring the pair of them—she left them to it.

'The doctor tells me you'll soon be as good as new.' She put on a cheerful face when she went straight up to see Stephanie.

'What else did he tell you?' Stephanie asked sharply.

Her tone warned Brooke that her sister had started to feel irritable again. 'Not a lot more,' she answered lightly, and truthfully. 'Jourdain Marchais joined us before I could ask Matthieu very much. I left them when they started to discuss something else.'

Stephanie did not ask what the something else had been, but suddenly she had taken a lightning change of mood, and her expression was definitely cheeky. '*Matth-ieu*, eh!' she exclaimed.

'Oh, shut up,' said Brooke, but had to grin at her sister's teasing.

Stephanie's mood was swift to change, however, and not five minutes later she was complaining of being bored to death. Relief was at hand, though. In the next minute Stephanie swung abruptly out of her mood, when Jourdain Marchais decided to look in on the invalid.

Not feeling very friendly towards him, Brooke made herself scarce and went down to the kitchen to prepare her own and Stepahnie's lunch tray.

Purposely she kept her thoughts away from Jourdain,

and knowing full well that Stephanie would be crawling up the wall with boredom soon after his visit was over, she concentrated her attention on what she could constructively do to relieve that boredom.

She decided there was nothing for it but to make a quick recce of the local shops. Luckily, she thought, she had changed some currency on the ferry. Then she remembered her father. Dearly did she want to know how his interview had gone, but, although the shock of seeing Stepahnie in the river was now past, Brooke could still not face phoning him. She had the idea of buying a picture postcard while she was at the shops, and sending it with some brief message that she was staying with Stephanie and her host for a few days, but then discarded it.

Laden with Stephanie's tray, Brooke left the kitchen. If things went her way, she mused, she and her sister might be home before any postcard she sent could reach him.

She turned into the wide hall, and, espying Emilie coming from the opposite direction, she had a greeting ready for when they passed each other.

Only they did not pass. For, as Brooke with her burden walked by the *salon* door, an explosive sound rent the air. Startled, she took a quick glance to the right, and was even more startled to see Jourdian standing there, the look on his face one of absolute fury.

Everything happened so quickly. One moment she had been holding Stephanie's tray, and the next, just as though his patience had been pushed to its limits, Jourdain had taken the tray from her, and Emilie had hold of it. Open-mouthed to see Emilie, under his curt instruction, move towards the stairs with the tray, Brooke was given no time to protest. For a firm hand on her arm had all but dragged her into the *salon*.

The force with which Jourdain closed the door told

her, in case she did not know it, that he was not well pleased about something. But neither was she, as she wrenched her arm from his hold.

'What the——' she started to errupt. It was as far as she got.

'Enough!' Jourdain roared. 'I have withstood enough!' and while Brooke floundered to know what he was talking about, he told her, 'I have ample fit and able staff. You will cease tripping up and down stairs the day long. Also you will keep out of the kitchen, and allow my staff to take your sister whatever she requires.'

Brooke was stung to be ordered to keep out of the kitchen, when she was sure Madame Lasserre had made no complaint to him, and pride began to mingle with her anger.

'Your staff have their own work,' she retorted. 'It isn't fair that they should have to fetch and carry for Stephanie, or me, when I, too, am perfectly fit and able.'

'Did you not understand me, *mademoiselle*?' That she was standing there arguing was not going down very well, Brooke saw.

'I understood you perfectly, *monsieur*,' she countered, 'but I still prefer to . . .'

He interrupted her abruptly, as his anger peaked and he thundered,

'Then understand this too, *mademoiselle*. Either you obey me, or I shall have Stephanie sent to hospital!'

'Hospital!' Brooke exclaimed, alarmed. 'But—but— Stephanie hates hospitals!'

What he would have answered, or if he would have said anything once victory was his, Brooke never discovered. For just then the phone on the bureau started to ring.

Reluctant to admit defeat, she glared impotently at him. But as he strode to answer the instistent ringing of the phone she knew that he considered their conversation at an end. She would be wasting her time if she hung around waiting for his call to end.

As angry with him as he was with her, she marched to the door. She was hotly unwilling to admit defeat, but even if he was bluffing, she knew she dared not call his bluff. Heaven knew what effect it would have on Stephanie if she was parcelled off to hospital.

Brooke had the door open and was halfway through it when Jourdain, his anger now under control, said, 'The call is for you, *mademoiselle*.'

Abruptly she swung about to see him holding the phone out to her. Her mind a momentary blank to know who would be telephoning her, she went forward and, without looking at him, took the receiver out of his hand.

'Hello,' she said, and suddenly, every scrap of anger left her. She was so surprised on recognising the voice that it passed her by entirely that although Jourdain had gone to the door, he had gone only to close it.

'I thought I'd better ring to check if you're keeping out of mischief, Stephanie,' teased her father's voice.

'Dad!' exclaimed Brooke in pleasure, and quickly told him, 'it's not Stephanie, it's Brooke.'

'Brooke!' he exclaimed in turn, and then chortled, 'well, well! I asked for Miss Farringdon, but . . . So you made it to Ecartéville, and looked Stephanie up?'

'That's right,' she said. It was then that her pleasure in hearing him so unexpectedly started to slide. Suddenly, she just knew she could not tell him anything about what had happened—not over the phone. He would worry too much. 'Actually,' she said, keeping her voice bright, 'I'm staying at the château with Stephanie for a few days.' Afraid he would start asking awkward questions about Stephanie before she was ready, Brooke went rattling on, 'When Monsieur Marchais knew I was in Normandy, he was kind enough to invite me to stay.'

'It's a nice place—this château?' he asked.

'Superb,' she told him, her voice softening, and she forgot everything for a few seconds as she tried to convey something of her feelings. 'It must truly be one of the most lovely places I've ever seen. The building itself is a dream, then there are fantastic gardens and trees. There's even a river that flows . . .' A spasm of anguish took her at the thought of the river and Stephanie, but she hurried on, 'But I'm more interested in how you got on in your interview. By the sound of your voice . . .'

'You've guessed it!' her father put in, obviously in top form. 'To tell the truth, that's really the reason I rang. I got my promotion, and I've been itching to tell someone, only there's nobody here I can tell.'

Oh, the dear love, Brooke thought, as she congratulated him. He must have been bubbling over inside to share his joy with someone, but not one of his children had been at home. They spoke for a minute or so about his promotion and the fact that it would take effect from the first of October, then Alec Farringdon asked,

'Where's the baby, by the way? Is she around?'

The fact that he still referred to Stephanie as the baby made her special. He loved her in spite of the maddening madam she could be at times, and this made Brooke more determined than ever to keep what had happened from him for as long as she could.

'She's around somewhere,' she told him cheerfully. 'But you know Stephanie, if I go to look for her where I think she'll be, ten to one she'll be somewhere else.'

'No need to get her,' Alec Farringdon replied. 'As long as she's all right . . .'

'Have you heard from Steven again?' Brooke butted in.

'No,' he replied, affection in his voice when he added,

'he'll roll up when he's ready—I suspect, both broke and starving.'

'Talking of starving,' Brooke did not allow a break in the conversation, 'are you eating enough? There should be sufficient in the freezer to last until I get home, but don't go ...'

'Er ...' her father cut in, and then, strangely, just as though he felt a degree uncomfortable about what he had to say, he coughed, cleared his throat, and told her, 'er—à propos not starving, I'm—er—taking a widow from one of the laboratories out to dinner tonight.'

As her father seldom went out of an evening and, so far as she knew, had absolutely no interest in the opposite sex, Brooke was too astonished to reply.

'You don't mind, do you?' he broke the small silence to ask quickly. 'I mean,' he defended, 'it's so quiet here without any of you around, and ...'

Swiftly Brooke came to terms with what her father had said, and as swiftly, broke in to tell him, 'Oh, Dad, I couldn't be more delighted!' Enthusiastically, as if he was Steven going out on his first date, she told him where he could find his other best shirt, and would have gone on to tell him to give his best suit a brush, when she checked herself. He would be forty-nine next birthday, for goodness' sake! 'Enjoy yourself, darling,' she told him instead, and in an attempt to ease his loneliness with all of them away, 'we—I,' she amended, quickly remembering that Stephanie had a few more weeks to go of the arrangement yet, 'will soon be home.'

A minute or two later, Brooke put down the phone. There was happiness in her and a hope, now her father had broken out of his mould, that he might begin to live life again. She knew nothing might come of just one date, but it was a start.

She turned from the bureau, and saw that Jourdain

was still in the room, but she was too pleased inside for the anger she had felt with him to return. His anger with her seemed to have evaporated too. Looking at her shining eyes, he remarked softly,

'You father's phone call has pleased you very much, Brooke.'

'Very much,' she replied. Forgetting how cross she had been with her host, she even smiled. 'Not only did he get his promotion, but, for the first time in the six years since my mother died, he's taking a lady out to dinner.'

'Your eyes, your expression, tell me you have no objection to—this new turn in his life.'

'None at all,' she smiled happily, then began to feel she had been a bit of an idiot to have babbled as she had about her father, and started to explain, 'he hardly ever goes out, so . . .'

'Speaking of going out,' Jourdain slipped in smoothly, 'have you been out in the fresh air since your sister fell into the river?'

Her feeling of euphoria had started to dip before he had changed the subject, and as his words sank in, her feeling of wellbeing disappeared completely.

'Fell, *monsieur*?' she enquired coldly, and saw what could have been a flicker of annoyance come to his eyes. It was quickly gone, but he did not let up on his question.

'Have you been out?' he persisted.

His persistence was starting to annoy *her*, but since he seemed determined she should answer him, she saw no reason not to let him into her plans.

'It's my intention to go "out", this afternoon,' she revealed coolly, and, not wishing to invite a third degree on where was she going, she added, 'staying in bed has always been a trial to Stephanie. I thought I'd go to the local shops to see if I can find something to relieve her boredom.'

She would have walked out of the *salon* then, but Jourdain's smile, his, 'I will take you to the village,' surprised her into remaining just where she was.

'Oh, there's no need,' she recovered quickly. 'I have my own car, and I'm sure I can easily find my way.'

'I'm sure you can,' he replied, showing the charm she had witnessed in him before. 'But can you *petite*, I wonder, ask for a—um—jigsaw puzzle in French? I envisage you may have one or two problems with my language.'

Brooke knew he was right, just as she knew that, although she did not want it to, his charm had somehow stifled the argumentative side of her. Certainly there was no argument left in her when, having waited long enough to counter anything she might have said, he placed a hand on her arm, led her to the door and told her,

'Please be ready at two.'

Strangely bemused by this turn of events, Brooke went slowly up the stairs. She was at Stephanie's door, when she acknowledged to herself that she did not mind too much the thought of going shopping with Jourdain.

'What happened to bring that excited look to your eyes?' was Stephanie's opening challenge when she went in.

Brooke flickered her glance from her, absently noting that the tray holding the salad she had prepared for her own lunch had been delivered to Stephanie's room. Her sister's jealous tone made her wary of telling her she had just come from a full assault of Jourdain's charm.

'Why shouldn't I be excited?' she queried as she took a seat in front of her lunch tray. 'Father's just phoned—his interview went well—he's been offered his own department.'

Stephanie's pleasure at the news matched her own, and while Brooke ate, she relayed much of the telephone

conversation. Aware that her young sister tended to be a
bit possessive in her relationships, she trod carefully
when she told her about her father's dinner date. But she
need not have worried, because Stephanie was wearing a
smile as she exclaimed,

'The old dog!' Then, as if she did not like the thought
that her father might have forgotten her, she questioned,
'Did he ask about me?'

'Of course he did. He rang to speak to you, in actual
fact, but I couldn't very well come and get you, with you
confined to bed. I—er—didn't tell him you were—
poorly,' Brooke added carefully. To her surprise, Stephanie agreed with her.

'Much better not,' she stated. 'You know what an old
hen he can be at times. The only reason he didn't want
me to come to France was because he thought I'd be too
far away if I got into any sort of pickle.'

To Brooke's mind, the moment was exactly right to
question her sister gently about the way she had tried to
drown herself. She wanted to help, and felt that only good
could come of getting Stephanie to talk it all out.

'Talking of pickles——' she began lightly.

'Don't!' snapped Stephanie, her smile soon replaced
by a disgruntled look. It was obvious she did not want to
discuss the emotional state she was in.

So Brooke didn't go on. She knew Stephanie. She knew
her asthma, and had to accept that unless she wanted her
all over-emotional again, when her breathing might too
easily become laboured, then for the moment the subject
was taboo.

'Okay,' she said easily. 'What would you like to talk
about?'

'Nothing,' was the sulky answer, followed by, 'I'm
bored.'

Stephanie's mood quickly changed, however, when

Brooke told her she thought she might venture to the shops to find something to relieve her bordeom. In less han no time she was directing her to bring back half a dozen items, which her sister simply could not do without.

A touch of guilt went through Brooke when on the dot of two, armed with her sister's shopping list, she went down the stairs. She had not told Stephanie that Jourdain was going with her. Somehow, in the face of her sister's jealousy, it had seemed better to keep quiet.

Jourdain was waiting for her, and courteously handed her into his car before he went round to the driver's side. He spoke little on the way, but seemed perfectly content to drive in silence.

The village was larger than she had anticipated, but lost none of its charm because of it. They parked outside a *charcuterie*, and while he secured the car Brooke looked her fill at the crammed window where long thin sausages hung down with fat squat sausages, and *terrines* of various pâtés lay side by side. Suddenly excitement and the rare feeling of rebellion she had felt two days before began to stir. She was in France. Was it wrong, if only for a brief while, that she should savour and enjoy the experience?

Her vision was taken up with the *rillettes* of pork and of salmon on display, when she became aware that Jourdain had come to stand close to investigate what held her with such rapt attention.

Unselfconsciously, she sent him a happy smile, and he smiled back. He appeared to have all day to spare, for he seemed in no hurry to take his glance from the curve of her mouth, and it occurred to Brooke then that she should be getting on, the sooner to get back to Stephanie.

She took the shopping list from her bag. 'Stephanie

needs . . .' she began, and had the list taken from her hand.

'Perhaps it will be simpler if I take charge of this,' he said softly, his eyes on hers as she looked up startled.

An undefined happiness, rooted somewhere in the heart of her, went with Brooke when Jourdain ushered her into a newsagents. That inner glow stayed when, together, they picked out magazines which might relieve some of Stephanie's boredom for a while. That glow grew when Jourdain spotted, of all things, a jigsaw puzzle, and comically held it up. Brooke could only nod, but at the laughter in his eyes she just had to burst out laughing herself.

Some of her happiness dimmed, however, when, at the cash desk, he would allow her to pay for none of the items they had selected together.

'But I insist!' she protested.

'Smile for me,' Jourdain answered, and paid whether she insisted or not.

At the next stop he again refused to allow her to pay. Brooke's happiness faded and she began to feel quite cross. For two pins she would have snatched the shopping list from him and had a go at making the next shopkeeper understand that she required to purchase hair spray and emery boards, but Jourdain gave her no chance.

The shopping list completed, Brooke had paid for not one single solitary item, and she was in no mood to smile when he escorted her back to the car—or to give him so much as a word of thanks when he again courteously saw that she was seated before he went to the driver's door.

Speak to him she did, though. For when, instead of slowing down to take the road she felt sure they had come along, he did nothing of the sort, but shot straight past, she was compelled to tell him coldly,

'You've missed the turn, *monsieur*.'

'I did not miss it,' he replied cheerfully. 'Did I not tell you, I have to pay a visit to one of the farms?'

He knew very well he hadn't told her, Brooke fumed silently. Frustrated at not being able to do anything about it, she was just about to ask how long his visit was going to take when, driving all urgent thoughts of getting back to Stephanie from her mind, he said suddenly,

'You manage to call my friend the doctor by his first name. So why, Brooke, am I still *"monsieur"* to you?'

If Jourdain had meant to take the wind out of her sails, then he had succeeded. For, if she had got it right, not only was he inviting her to use his first name, but she had offended him, by not yet doing so!

She had formed the opinion that no matter which way she jumped, it would be the wrong way, when Jourdain pulled up at the farm he was to visit. Determination to stay put vied with good manners when he came round and opened the passenger door. Good manners won. Offending him had become a habit, so she was not too concerned about offending him again, but to show bad manners and offend him in front of his tenants was something she could not do.

Their visit would not take too long, though, she discovered, for Jourdain's knock at the door was not answered.

'You'll be able to phone when you get home,' she suggested, starting to feel more even-tempered.

'Oh, they won't be far away,' Jourdain pronounced, and to knock on the head any idea that they would now go back to the château, 'we'll take a short walk while we wait.'

Brooke looked at where the car stood baking in the afternoon sun. Since he had the car keys, even if she could get the electronically operated windows down, it

would still be like an oven in there without the air-
conditioning on. She looked from the car to where a line
of trees sheltered a footpath, and common sense won.

The path was narrow, and caused her to have to walk
fairly close to her host. Had she thought their short stroll
would be completed in silence, she discovered her
mistake early on.

'The weather is beautiful, don't you think?' Jourdain
opened.

'Are you ribbing me?' answered Brooke, sure he had
his tongue very much in his cheek.

'Ribbing you?' he enquired, for all the world as if he
didn't know what she was talking about.

Brooke had always found something rather splendid
about trees, and could only suppose that this tree-lined
leafy walk was having a weakening effect on her.
Because suddenly she found she was playing along with
him.

'I thought it was only the British who had a mania for
talking about the weather.'

'From my experience on visits to your country,' he
replied lightly, his charm still there beneath the surface,
'I would suggest your weather is not worth comment.'

Amused by this answer, she could hardly control a
smile. 'You needn't sound so smug,' she told him, her
voice giving away the smile she tried to suppress, 'it
rained here non-stop when I arrived.'

'Yet you still found the area beautiful,' he answered,
and reminded her when she cast a querying look at him,
'I overheard you tell your father, with truth in your voice,
how beautiful you find my home.'

What could she say? 'Guilty,' she pleaded.

'Perhaps,' said Jourdain, when they had strolled on a
few more yards, 'since you enjoy the beauty of the
château and the grounds so much, you might like to delay

your departure.'

There had been no hint of what was coming. Startled, Brooke bumped into him. His hand was quickly on her arm to steady her, and remained there when she tried to edge away from him.

'You're suggesting,' she began when she had got her breath back, 'I prolong my—er—er—holiday?' She couldn't get over it. 'But you don't want me here!' she gasped.

'When did I ever say anything of the sort?' Jourdain challenged.

'Well, you might not have said it,' she had to confess, 'but . . .' She broke off, and sensing she was going to be on the losing side of any argument, settled for, 'What does it matter? As soon as Stephanie is well enough to travel, I shall be taking her home.'

When the hand on her arm fell away, she knew his mood had changed. There was none of the charm he had so far shown her, quite the opposite in fact, when he questioned sharply,

'You have some—man—you want to get back to, *mademoiselle*?'

She had two men to get back to, her father who was just as likely to wear odd socks if she wasn't there to pair them up for him, and Steven who she wanted to ensure was scrubbed, washed and pressed before she sent him off to university.

'Yes,' she replied, and thought that was all the answer needed to satisfy him. She found she was wrong again. They had walked on to where the path ended and where trees were interspersed with a grassy area when, quite savagely, she thought, Jourdain grated,

'He can't be much of a man—this Englishman. You still have your virginity.'

'Some men,' Brooke flung straight back, 'have more

respect than to want a girl to . . .' she started to flounder, '. . . to go against her values and—and give herself to s-satisfy a—a man's momentary—er—lust.'

His hand on her arm again halted her. Angrily, she looked up and saw he appeared faintly incredulous to have heard her state such an old-fashioned viewpoint.

'Mon Dieu!' he exclaimed, but recovered to toss at her, 'what sort of man have you that he cannot stir the passion I have seen in you, and make you forget everything, but that you want to give yourself to him?'

'Oh, for goodness' sake!' Brooke erupted. The man they were speaking of was unknown to her, but that did not prevent her from bestowing on him a certain set of principles. 'He's a man who would certainly never creep up on a girl and kiss her while she was asleep.' She added, as a way to defend her subsequent response suddenly occurred to her, 'Nor would he continue to kiss her when she was still half asleep with no clear idea of what she was doing!'

Jourdain looked at her for long seconds, his glance sceptical. Then his expression changed, but Brooke liked the smile that came to his face none the better. Nor did she care for the silky way in which he asked,

'Would you say—you are fully awake now?'

Warily she nodded, but her heart jerked a nervous beat when the hand on her arm glided smoothly round her back. Too late, she realised she should have shaken her head. For even as she made a move to jerk away from him, his head was coming down.

The iron bar of his arm made her attempt to get free ineffective. She felt his mouth on her own, and her heart fluttered another nervous beat. She tried hard to push him away, but her efforts only resulted in his other arm coming around her as he secured her closer to him.

Brooke continued to push at him. She did not want to

feel the warmth which emanated from him. She did not want his arms about her. She did not want to his kiss, gentle though it was. She did not want . . .

Her thoughts grew confused, his mouth was gently teasing her lips apart. Her heart gave a nerv . . . no, an excited beat, and something odd was happening to her.

Jourdain's mouth left hers, but she did not cry out. She could not cry out. His mouth was whispering tender kisses on her cheek, and she leaned against him, her legs suddenly weak. As Jourdain trailed kisses down her cheek, moving down to her throat, Brooke's arm moved, holding tightly on to him, as if afraid she would fall.

A flame of fire started somewhere inside her. Then, as though she was made of fragile glass, she felt Jourdain move her, move with her, and take her with him down to the carpet of grass. She opened her eyes without realising she had closed them, and Jourdain, his look caring, smiled at her. Brooke smiled back, and he kissed her again.

Under the shade of a large oak tree, she lay with him. She felt his body warmth when he lay half over her, felt his kiss strengthening, searching, until he found an answering response.

Jourdain's lips tormented the swollen fullness of the mouth she offered him, and as he pressed closer to her, her body answered that pressure.

His mouth took hers, and suddenly she never wanted him to leave her. Desperately she clung to him, his name, 'Jourdain,' leaving her lips when his mouth left hers. His hands cupped her face, and he kissed her eyes. Then his hands left her face and caressed her shoulders. The neck of her dress parted and her body vibrated with the pleasure he gave her.

His mouth came to hers again, and his hands caressed her shoulders and beyond. She wanted him to touch her, yet when his right hand captured her left breast, she could not hold back on a spasm of movement. No man had held her breast before.

'Relax, *mignonne*,' Jourdain whispered throatily, 'I shall not harm you.'

A held in breath left her, and Brooke relaxed—she wanted more.

He continued to fondle her breast, and a moan of wanting left her. Her bodice buttons were undone, and she felt the warmth of his hand as gentling her, it slipped unhurriedly inside her bra.

'Jourdain,' his name came on a quickened breath from her tongue.

He moved from her, and a sigh left her as she knew he had only moved in order to bend his head to kiss her breast in his hand. Then he raised his head, and his mouth captured hers while his finger tips tormented her so that she was beside herself with her need.

Her desire for him mounted and she just had to feel his skin too. He helped her unbutton his shirt and, with at first tentative fingers, she sought inside it.

Minutes went by as he aroused her to a mindless wanting. Aware all the time of his caressing hands, she noticed acutely when his hands left her breasts and returned to touch her, but not where they had been.

In her wonder at the gentleness of his lovemaking, shyness had taken very little part, when suddenly it took over.

She wanted him, and knew she should not back away when his hand moved to the skirt of her dress. She did not want to retreat, but while there was excited flame at the feel of his touch on her thighs, at the same time she also felt agitated. She tried to control her agitation as Jourdain kissed her and his hand caressed up to her hip. As she kissed him back, she felt his touch at the top of her briefs, and tried, as he had instructed, to relax. But when his hand ventured further, with a strangled, 'No—I can't!' she sprang away from him.

She was on her feet, straightening her clothing, by the time Jourdain had unwound his long length to stand beside her. She had no idea whether he was angry with her, or how she expected him to feel. What she did not expect, however, was that he would be so calm, so unruffled. With a shrug just as if he had thought 'Win some—lose some' and had put her down to experience, he stated quietly,

'No one asked you to, *chérie*.'

'You . . .' She had been going to argue—you did! But he hadn't. Apart from that first kiss, and maybe the second she had met him all the way. He had been ready to take, she was sure of that, but he appeared not the slightest put out that she had given—only so far. Most peculiarly, that annoyed her.

'You seem to be having trouble with your buttons,' Jourdain murmured, witnessing the hash her shaking fingers were making of getting her dress done up. 'Allow me,' he said, still in that same unruffled voice.

'Don't you dare touch me!' Brooke spat, the calm she had at one time been able to call up at will having no chance in this moment of crisis. Angry, if not certain whom she was angry with, she knocked his hands away. Suddenly her emotions were in too much of an uproar, and buttoning up her dress as she went, she took to her heels and ran.

She did not care then whether she was being irrational, or what she was being. Prior to coming to France she had always been cool, calm and collected. Now look at her! Jourdain Marchais had done this to her, and she—knowing in advance what a flirt he was—had let him!

She saw his car standing where he had left it, but

though a stitch in her side made her slow down, she walked past it. She had no idea how far it was back to the château, but since it had not taken very long to get to the farm, it couldn't be so far that she couldn't walk it.

She was nearing the end of the farm drive when a car drew up alongside her. It wasn't her day. Trust her to walk on the driver's side! The car window came down.

'Get in, Brooke,' Jourdain commanded. She ignored him, and kept on walking. He drove beside her. 'I know you're upset,' he continued evenly, 'and I can understand it has come as a shock to know that you wanted me, as I wanted you . . .'

He broke off and braked as Brooke halted, stock-still. It offended her that he should bring matters out into the open, but since he had, she told him acidly, 'You want everything in a skirt!'

She turned her head, and was about to march on, when a stout lady of mature years—one of the stoutest she had ever seen—waddled in front of the car.

'Not everything, *ma petite*,' she heard Jourdain murmur, and knew that his eyes must have followed hers.

To her annoyance, his words made her lips twitch, which contrarily caused her to turn her head to show him a haughty look. Only it didn't come off, for Jourdain had witnessed her attempt not to laugh, and she saw he was smiling.

'Call me a French flirt, call me what you will,' he said, 'but Stephanie is waiting for her jigsaw puzzle.'

Consumed by guilt that she had forgotten all about Stephanie, Brooke promptly gave in. She got into the car beside him.

She was too preoccupied with her own thoughts to ponder what occupied him on that silent return to the château. No sooner had he pulled up than, not waiting for him to come round and open her door, she had seized her parcels up in her arms and was out of the car like a shot. She was still mentally at sixes and sevens when she went into her sister's room.

'You took your time!' Stephanie greeted her peevishly, obviously not pleased at the length of time she had been away. 'Did you walk *both* ways?' she asked. The jealous note was there in her voice again. 'I thought I just heard Jourdain's car.'

Her sister's question showed she believed she had walked to the village, but suddenly Brooke felt too weary to want to try to explain anything. There were some things she could not explain even to herself.

'He gave me a lift,' she replied, and putting her parcels down on Stepahnie's bed, felt a need to be on her own.

'Did he kiss you again?' Stephanie would not let up. For once Brooke ran out of patience.

'Don't be tiresome, Stephanie!' she told her sharply, and headed for the door.

When Brooke reached the sanctuary of her own room she had to confess to a feeling of being very mixed up. Jourdain Marchais had turned all her beliefs about the type of person she was upside down. Given that he made her more angry at times than she had thought possible, she had to own that she would far rather be with him than with her sister!

CHAPTER SEVEN

STEPHANIE looked askance at the jigsaw puzzle, but the rest of the purchases went some way to relieve her bordom. Brooke had dinner with her, and went to bed that night without having clapped eyes on Jourdain again.

She was up early the next morning, and found that Stephanie, after a sound night's rest, was breathing normally and appeared to be as well as she had ever been. But the day did not start well. Any hopes that in regaining her health Stephanie might have recovered her good humour were soon dashed.

'You're looking bright-eyed and bushy-tailed,' Brooke told her cheerfully as she plumped up her pillows. Stephanie was unresponsive. 'We'll soon have you sitting out of bed at this rate,' she pressed on encouragingly.

'I'm not sitting out anywhere,' Stephanie muttered into her chin, 'until I've discussed it with Jourdain.'

'Jourdain!' Brooke exclaimed, unthinking until, her heart dropping, she saw how crazy her sister must be about the man. 'You—don't think perhaps Dr Delage might be the better person to . . .'

'No, I don't,' snapped Stephanie, but with a hint that she was fed up to the back teeth with bed. 'Anyway, the wretched man is away today, and won't be calling.'

From then on things went from bad to worse, with Stephanie looking for the least excuse to grumble, and Brooke at her wits' end to know what to do to take her out of her grim mood.

At one stage Brooke felt her patience start to fray, and

fearing she might say something short and sharp—which would help neither of them—she left Stephanie and went to her own room. She spent a few minutes in tidying around, then, her equilibrium restored, she opened the door intending to go back. Stephanie's laughter, through her open door, halted her.

Her nerves starting to jump, Brooke waited only long enough to hear Jourdain's French tones before ducking back inside. She could not face seeing him. She did not re-emerge until a good five minutes after her listening ears told her he had ended his visit and had gone past her door and down the stairs.

There was no sign of laughter about Stephanie when Brooke joined her. Although to start with she had forgotten to be argumentative, it did not last. At twelve-thirty, thinking she had better go to her room to re-charge her patience batteries again, Brooke made some excuse, and heard that Stephanie, the very devil in her, was like-minded.

'Don't hurry back on my account,' her sister pouted sulkily.

'I won't,' Brooke retorted, and got out before similar sharp words could escape her.

Ten minutes later, Brooke was being plagued by remorse and wanting quite desperately to go home. At home, she knew and understood the person she was. Here, since coming to the château, she had met in herself a person she did not recognise. The same, she thought, could be said for Stephanie, because never—ill or well— had she known her to be such a perverse little madam.

Remorse started to dig deep that she had allowed her curly-headed sister's perversity to drive her near to losing patience with her. Brooke didn't like herself very much. She was just wondering how she could have let herself forget how Stephanie, her emotions upset, had tried to do

away with herself, when the sound of a car tearing
furiously up the drive and coming to a screeching halt
stopped all thought.

Certain that Jourdain would never drive like that, not
unless there was something terribly wrong, Brooke
hurried to the window. It was not Jourdain, nor was it his
car.

The car was some sports model, its occupant female.
When a slim, elegant dark-haired young woman left the
car and stood on the forecourt, Brooke was satisfied that
there was no emergency, but she did not come away from
the window. For suddenly, as Jourdain emerged from the
building, and the elegant young woman fairly hurled
herself into his arms, the most violent feelings rioted in
Brooke, making her incapable of movement.

A second later, feeling a pain such as she had never felt
before at seeing Jourdain with his arms around another
woman, Brooke staggered back. She groped for a chair
and closed her eyes, but the image of Jourdain with the
young woman wrapped in his arms would not go away.

Brooke knew before she had put a label to the emotion
which assaulted her that she was in love with Jourdain
Marchais. She knew as she labelled that emotional pain
jealousy, that, although Jourdain was the last person she
would have chosen to fall in love with, she could not deny
the shattering truth of that love.

Shaken to her depths, she had in no way recovered
when, only a minute later, it seemed, the maid Grace
brought her a note. With difficulty, Brooke remembered
her manners. '*Merci*, Grace,' she thanked her, but she
had not the wit to think of reading what the note said and
asking the maid to wait for an answer, if there was to be
one, until after she had gone.

When she did get around to reading it, the note was
brief, couched in courteous terms, which held a

command none the less. It was from Jourdain. He had a guest, he informed her—as if she did not know—and would she please do him the politeness of joining him and his guest for lunch.

Her first reaction was, no, never. The last thing she wanted was to watch him flirt with his lady-love. She'd be damned if she'd play gooseberry ... Her thoughts started to falter. Why on earth did Jourdain want her to join him and his guest for lunch today, when up until now it had not bothered him where she ate her meals?

It did not take her long to work out the answer. It all boiled down to honour and manners, she saw quickly. Plainly his visitor knew of the existence of his other guests. But while Stephanie's absence could be excused on the grounds that she was bed-bound, his other house-guest could be guilty of offending him and his lady-friend by not coming to the table.

Quite obviously he had seen for himself that Stephanie looked well and would come to no harm if she had her lunch without her sister. Equally obviously, honour and good manners meant a lot to Jourdain.

For perhaps two minutes more, Brooke thought she would be quite happy to offend Jourdain Marchais, and not care a hoot if she offended his lady-love into the bargain, But inbred good manners, not to mention some latent masochistic desire to take a close look at the sort of female Jourdain's taste ran to, then began to stir in her.

Sixty seconds later, she was tearing around to do what she could in the short time available, to give herself something approaching the elegance of his other luncheon guest.

Deciding she looked more neat and tidy in her pink linen than in *haute couture*, Brooke left her room.

Half an hour ago she would have ignored her sister's 'Don't hurry back' and would have popped in to see her.

But that was earlier. Brooke went straight on down the stairs. If she was to present herself in the dining room for one o'clock she had little time to look in on Stephanie. Besides during the last half hour, emotions of such strength had besieged Brooke that her sister being bloody-minded, just for the sake of it, paled into insignificance.

When Brooke walked into the *salle-à-manger*, Jourdain was standing in conversation with the most ravishing creature, a few years younger than herself.

'Ah, Brooke!' he turned to her, a well-mannered smile on his face as he came up to her, his eyes on the warm colour that memory of their last meeting brought to her face.

There was no sign that he remembered how passionately they had kissed, Brooke thought. As her colour subsided and Jourdain drew her towards his companion, she felt quite ill with jealousy, and knew she was not going to be able to eat a thing. Then suddenly she was shattered for the second time that day—and this time delightfully so. For, unbelievably, Jourdain said,

'Allow me to introduce my niece, Mélisande ...' Emotional shock and relief sent Brooke deaf as he completed the introductions, but she had a few moments to get herself together a little while Jourdain told Mélisande how his English guest was not fully conversant with their tongue.

Her smile was as sunny as the day as she shook hands with Mélisande. Nor could Brooke deny the warm glow she experienced when, just as if she was some very special guest, Jourdain guided her to the table and pulled out her chair.

Common sense, however, relegated that glow to its proper place as soon as she was seated. She knew then that she had better start putting a check on her fantasies before they began. Courtesy came as second nature to Jourdain—she must be an utter idiot to imagine she would ever be special 'anything' where he was concerned.

Although she gave herself a short talking-to, the glow returned when, throughout the meal, the talk was solely in English, and not once did Jourdain exclude her from the conversation.

He could be forgiven, she thought, for occasionally lapsing into a brief mention to Mélisande of people they both knew, but neither friends nor family were discussed. In fact, Brooke was the one to mention family when she enquired of Mélisande how her father was.

'He is much improved,' Mélisande told her with a smile. 'He has one more test, but the—um—prognosis, yes?' she enquired the word of her uncle, and at his nod, 'looks to be good,' she added, and volunteered, 'when the last test is complete, both my parents will come here to rest, and holiday, and, as my *oncle* says, "keep me in order".' She sent a cheeky grin to Jourdain.

Brooke smiled at this intimation that, despite Mélisande's elegance, she was as giddy as Stephanie. The meal was progressing to an end, when Mélisande, who gave the impression, her mad driving included, that she was never still for long, put down her serviette, and asked to be excused.

'I must go and say *bonjour* to poor Stephanie!' she exclaimed. As Brooke made a movement to get to her feet she added cheerily, 'Perhaps if I sit with her for some time, it will give you an opportunity to take some fresh air.'

Maybe because Jourdain had enquired yesterday if she had been out, Brooke's eyes went to him, and met his gaze full on. She saw him start to smile, and hastily looked away, the memory of how that 'fresh air' had affected her yesterday causing her some moments of confusion.

She looked at Mélisande instead, and could not miss the curiosity with which the girl glanced at both her and Jourdain. Oh, grief, throught Brooke, wishing she was the sort of person who could be party to a passionate interlude and think no more about it. She felt sure that Mélisande suspected something had gone on, or was going on, between her and Jourdain. In her confusion, Brooke was afraid that anything she said would be wrong.

Jourdain, however, came swiftly in to tease his niece about her driving, and saved Brooke from having to say anything. 'I should go now, *petite*,' he said easily. 'Stephanie—like the whole of Ecartéville, I shouldn't wonder—will have heard you arrive, and will want to see you.'

Mélisande's curiosity faded under a grin. 'I'll see you later, Brooke,' she said, and left them.

Brooke had got over her confusion but, just as she realised how happy she had been throughout lunch, her happiness vanished. As sanity returned she was to remember that she had only been invited to the table because good manners decreed. Only then was she able to see that the reason no mention of people Mélisande or Jourdain knew, family or friends, was not from regard for her, but because they thought of her as an outsider.

She needed to get out of the room fast because of the dreadful feeling that she might burst into foolish tears of hurt at any moment. Brooke managed to mumble, 'Excuse me,' and left her chair.

What she did not need, as she made for the door, was for Jourdain to call her name to halt her. Instinct urged her onward, but pride would not allow her to give away the fact that there was anything amiss. She swallowed hard, then turned. He too had left the table, she saw, and had come to stand barely a yard away. She gave him her best enquiring look.

'May I take you for a drive?' he asked casually, and, as her anger triumphed over her weepy feeling, Brooke very nearly blew it there and then.

It seemed to her that everyone appeared to think she was in need of great dollops of fresh air. But, whether Jourdain Marchais, ever the flirt, thought to climax their 'drive' with another passionate interlude, or was merely making a further display of his courtesy to a guest, she didn't thank him.

'No, *monsieur*,' she told him coldly, 'you may not.'

She saw from the sudden thrust of his jaw that he didn't thank her for her cold refusal either. But when it came to cutting the ground from under her, he had no equal. His arrogance returned in full when, rocking slightly back on his heels, he enquired coolly,

'Am I to understand, *mademoiselle*, that you will only use my first name in your more—passionate—moments?'

How I hate him! Brooke thought as she stormed away—but her heart said differently. She gained the top of the stairs to be greeted by gales of laughter coming from Stephanie's room. She went to her own room with the thought that it seemed everyone but her could make Stephanie laugh.

Totally and utterly dejected, Brooke looked out of her window hoping the view she had found so much joy in might cheer her up. She did not see the view, though. What she did see was the back of Jourdain's car as it sailed down the drive.

Good, she thought, and, since everyone thought she should have some air, she decided to take a walk.

Despite her wish not to have him there, Jourdain was

in her mind when she descended the stairs and slipped out of a side exit. She had still not come to terms with the knowledge that she loved him, as she went absently where chance took her.

She walked along the river bank amidst the trees she loved, thoughts of Stephanie penetrating when she looked at the water. Oh God, what a mess, she sighed inwardly. She had come here to rescue her sister from the man Stephanie believed herself in love with, only to find that, far from rescuing her, she had fallen in love with the man herself!

Brooke walked on, and coming to a sawn-off tree trunk, she sat down to mull over how love made a normally logical head illogical. For, in that idyllic spot, in the shade of tall stately trees, she knew that while logic urged that the only thing to be done was to go home, she did not want to go.

Sadness, a dull, unhappy companion, sat with her when she tried to come to terms with the fact that she must leave this beautiful place. Time passed while she took in all she could remember when she had left.

She had no idea how long she had been away from the château when she finally left her seat. What she did know as she made her way back was that while she could and would leave Jourdain's home, it would break her heart to leave him.

Still intent on taking her fill of the scene, Brooke retraced her steps, noting absently on the way the care which went into the maintenance of the grounds. She guessed her head must have been too full when she had come this way earlier, because only now did it register that fresh gravel, which had not been there a couple of days ago, had been laid on the river path.

She entered the château by the same door from which she had left it. As she crossed the hall, thinking it was about time she looked in on her sister, Mélisande came tripping out of the *salon*.

'There you are!' she exclaimed, her smile there instantly. 'You are just in time for tea.'

'I was going up to see Stephanie,' Brooke smiled back.

'Oh, but I have ordered English tea and cakes especially for you,' Mélisande said prettily. 'It is all ready in the *salon*.'

In the face of such an invitation Brooke thought it churlish to refuse. 'Thank you, Mélisande,' she accepted, and went towards her, thinking Stephanie wouldn't mind if she didn't see her for another ten minutes.

Mélisande stepped back to allow her to procede her into the *salon*, and Brooke had begun to explain. 'I've been taking a walk by the . . .' when surprise at seeing Jourdain, taking his ease in the *salon*, made her break off.

'You enjoyed your walk, Brooke?' he enquired smoothly, courteously rising and waiting until she was seated before he resumed his seat.

'Er—very much,' she answered, and with a devil pushing her to let him know that it was not only his heady love making that could wrench his name from her, she calmly added, 'Jourdain'.

She did not see what his reaction was, although she hardly thought he was cut to the quick. Mélisande handing her a cup of tea and offering the cake stand gave Brooke something else to concentrate on.

The younger girl kept up a lively conversation, and if Brooke wondered why Jourdain had deigned to join them over the English teacups, then the obvious family affection between the two gave her the answer. Also, Jourdain would no doubt consider it bad manners to leave his niece too much alone on her first day back.

Her teacup empty, Brooke had just refused another cup, thinking that with all the politeness observed, she could now leave the *salon*, when Mélisande suddenly lapsed back into French, and was reminded by Jourdain to speak in English.

'I'm sorry,' she apologised straight away, with more than a touch of her uncle's charm. 'With Stephanie fluent in French, I forgot for a little moment that you are not.' Her smile joined her charm when, as though to make Brooke feel easier about her sister, she went on, 'Speaking of Stephanie, there appears to me to be nothing the matter with her.'

Only a moment before Jourdain had reminded her to speak in English, so it was strange when he spoke sharply to his niece in French. Brooke supposed she must have looked her surprise, for when Jourdain transferred his gaze from Mélisande to her, it was his turn to smile.

'It must be contagious,' he excused, and explained, 'I was just telling this young lady that, since she was not here to see Stephanie when first she was taken ill, you would think her comments extremely rude.'

'Not at all,' murmured Brooke, her glance going to Mélisande who was looking at them with the same light of curiosity in her eyes that had been there before. That curiosity had gone though, when she asked,

'I am forgiven for my rudeness, Brooke?'

Brooke had not thought her rude, merely truthful. For the tablets Stephanie was taking had worked such wonders, she did now look as though there was nothing the matter with her.

'There's nothing to forgive,' Brooke told her, and thanked her for the tea. Then she left her chair and was on her way. It had not occurred to her that Jourdain would go to the door and open it for her, but he did. When she flicked a glance at him and murmured a polite, 'Thank you,' she saw that the smile he had worn a short while ago had gone.

'You will oblige me by joining me for dinner this evening, Brooke,' he stated quietly, his expression almost stern.

She opened her mouth to say no, but could not. Even with Mélisande there as well, she wanted to be with Jourdain at his dinner-table tonight. Soon she would go home, never to see him again.

'Of course,' she replied. Her heart was bumping erratically just to be standing so close to him, and this time she could not add his name. Swiftly she turned and walked away.

Her heartbeats had evened out by the time she reached her sister's room. Too late she realised that, by putting what she wanted first for once, she had completely forgotten how Stephanie was going to take it!

'Where have you been?' was the first question to hit her ears when Stephanie saw her.

'Out for a walk,' Brooke replied evenly, but she was glad to note that, if not exactly smiling, Stephanie looked nowhere near as cantankerous as she had been.

'You've seen Mélisande?'

'I met her at lunch, and we've just had a cup of tea together.'

'She's great, isn't she?' Stephanie enthused, and taking her agreement for granted, 'Did you see that suit she had on? I'm going the get one like that.'

Stephanie's conversation from then on was more what it used to be. For the next half an hour, clothes, or her lack of them, were the main topic.

'I suppose I'd better go and see what I can rustle up in the chic line myself.' Brooke trod on eggs, as she drew near to telling her sister that it would be a dinner tray for one that night. 'I'm expected to dine downstairs tonight, and I shouldn't want Mélisande to think I'm—to use your expression—from Hicksville,' she hurried on.

To Brooke's surprise, not to say relief, instead of throwing a sulk at this news, Stephanie was completely on her side. 'I'll bet Mélisande will wear something absolutely stunning,' she opined, then asked thoughtfully, 'I don't suppose you thought to bring your black velvet with you?'

'I—er—did, actually,' answered Brooke, having packed the calf-length black velvet dress purely and simply because, with its swathes of tissue, it had helped to fill the large suitcase her father had insisted she packed.

'Good,' said Stephanie, and made Brooke's dress sense shudder, when she added. 'there's a shocking pink chiffon scarf in that drawer over there. If you drape it artistically around the neck, it'll look a wow.'

To keep her sister happy, Brooke fetched the pink chiffon from the drawer, but she knew she wouldn't wear it unless she was going to some fancy dress do.

She took the scarf with her to her room and saw that she just had time to wash her fine hair and get it dry by dinner-time. Never before had she taken any man into consideration when she dressed, but Brooke wanted to look her best that night.

At a quarter to eight, she studied her reflection in the full-length mirror. The black velvet seemed to give an added something to her fair skin. With the intention of dropping the scarf back into her room later, she draped it around the neck of her dress and went in to see her sister.

'I'm not sure about the scarf now,' was Stephanie's opinion. 'Take it off and let's have a look.' Brooke duly obliged. 'Hmm. That's more you, I think,' was her considered opinion. 'You're not going to outshine Mélisande, but you'll do. You didn't bring Mother's pearls with you, I suppose?'

'As a matter of fact, I didn't,' Brooke replied, more

cheered than she could say that Stephanie appeared to be out of her ill-humour. 'You're pleased Mélisande is back, aren't you?' she asked.

Stephanie nodded. 'She's a real scream,' she told her, 'and such good company when Jourdain goes away.'

'He—goes away often?' Brooke enquired carefully, wanting to know all she could about him.

'I'm sure I told you he had other business interests to keep an eye on,' Stephanie said seriously. 'In fact, I expected him to tootle off this week. I know he had a meeting in Paris scheduled for Friday.' She smiled then, an arch sort of smile, and gave a dramatic sigh when she declared, 'No doubt my being ill made him decide to cancel it.'

'No doubt,' Brooke agreed, and as the time was going on, she added, 'I'll look in later,' and left her sister.

Her heart had already begun to pick up an excited beat at the thought that she would soon see Jourdain again. She was halfway down the stairs when a movement made her halt. Jourdain, immaculate in a lounge suit, was standing at the bottom looking up at her.

Her heart suddenly began to race, and searching for calm, Brooke gripped the banister hard before she carried on down the stairs. Jourdain did nothing to help her retain any calm she had found when, as she reached him, he looked down into her eyes, took hold of her arm, and murmured,

'You are very, very lovely, Brooke.'

Confusion was too small a word for what she felt then, as, in a daze, she allowed him to guide her to the outside door. Even if it had occurred to her that the outside door was a peculiar way to go to the dining-room, she would probably not have said anything.

As it was, Jourdain had led her outside and handed her into his car before she came to her senses and realised that, vast though the château was, surely, if they were dining in some other part of his home, they would not need a car to drive there?

'What—where . . .?' she spluttered, but the car was drawing away from the château by the time she had got herself sorted out. 'Where are you taking me?' she finally got the words out in one sentence.

'Out to dine,' Jourdain replied easily, and steered the car out of the drive and into the lane beyond.

'Out to d-dine!' She was spluttering again. 'But—but . . .'

'You need a night off, *ma petite*,' Jourdain said in soft soothing tones. 'You . . .'

'No, I don't,' she tried to argue.

'Yes, you do,' he said calmly, as the car accelerated under the pressure of his foot. 'I asked you to dine with me, do you not remember?'

Winded, Brooke could only remember that he had stated she would dine with him. But she had thought Méli . . . 'Where's Mélisande?' she managed to ask, though she was still in shock.

'I did not ask her to join us,' Jourdain replied in that same calm voice.

She was stunned as it dawned on her that Jourdain had suspected she would refuse to leave the château if he had gone about it any other way. The car sped on. Speechless, Brooke came to the realisation that—for as long as it took them to eat dinner anyway—she had been virtually kidnapped!!

CHAPTER EIGHT

ANGER mixed with shock that, in order to ensure she had a night off, away from Stephanie's beck and call, Jourdain should take it upon himself to kidnap her from the château. But from what little she knew of him, Brooke knew she would be wasting her time to demand that he turn the car around and head straight back.

She was still fairly stunned when he pulled up in front of another château.

Brooke had maintained a stony silence throughout the drive. Yet she could not deny a flicker of interest to note that this building was not a private house like the château Jourdain owned, but had been turned into a hotel.

The cool outside air brushed her cheeks when Jourdain came round and opened the passenger door. Her curiosity to see the inside of the hotel was at odds with a determination not to give in to his high-handed treatment. She made no move to get out.

'Are you so very cross with me that you can turn your back on the delicious meal that awaits you?' asked Jourdain, his voice coaxing and full of charm.

'You—shouldn't have done it,' mumbled Brooke, still stubbornly not moving.

'But why?' he asked, a warm note there. 'You are so used to doing things for others—cannot you allow me the honour to do some small thing for you?'

His charm alone started her stubbornness crumbling. His words, the fact—even if he did not mean it—that Jourdain had stated that it would be an honour to do something for her made her backbone begin to wilt. It was only dinner after all, prompted a small voice to which she suddenly wanted to listen. It would only be for a short while, and had she not wanted to spend some time with him?

'W-will—Stephanie be all right?' she asked hesitantly.

Jourdain bent into the car and set her pulses racing as his face close to hers, he smiled and placed a hand on her arm. 'Would I leave her without a companion.' he asked softly. 'Our two relatives get on well together, do they not?'

Without realising she had moved, Brooke found he had gently pulled her from the car. He was tall beside her, good-looking, and Brooke's heart knew a thrill at the thought of having him for her escort. What could she do? She went with him into the château-cum-hotel.

They were expected, she discovered. Jourdain was well known to the smart, efficient lady who ran the establishment, and who came and shook hands with them both.

Brooke found her lost smile surfaced naturally. Although Madame Dumont spoke no English, her welcome for her was as warm as it had been for Jourdain. Madame Dumont personally led them to an ante-room, where Jourdain courteously guided Brooke to a plush two-seater settee. He had a few more words with Madame Dumont, who went quickly on her way, and when he took the seat beside Brooke, she promptly felt a need to say something—anything.

'The—this hotel was once a château, wasn't it?' she asked.

Jourdain nodded. 'Unfortunately,' he told her, 'the upkeep of old property is a constant drain on resources. When Madame Dumont came to a financial crisis, it was either sell—which she could not consider—or find a way to make the château pay for itself.'

Just then the head waiter appeared with a couple of aperitifs which Brooke guessed Jourdain must have ordered, at the same time handing them each a menu.

Putting the glass of sherry on a low table in front of her, Brooke opened her leather-bound menu—and was immediately lost. It was written entirely in French. Jourdain saw her predicament at once. When he bent his head near hers to translate, she knew she would have to try and get some control from somewhere—just his nearness making her feel dizzy.

'Oh,' she said, needing to grab at anything that had some touch on normality to it. 'There aren't any prices on my menu, but there are on yours,' She felt ridiculous as soon as she had said it, but Jourdain made her feel instantly better, when he pronounced,

'Which is just as it should be.'

'Is it—fearfully expensive here?' she questioned, thinking that, since Jourdain too had a château to keep up, he could well be as hard-pressed as Madame Dumont had been.

'Not—*fearfully*,' he teased, the warm smile in his grey eyes doing funny things to her inside. Then he was serious all at once. She had thought that in regard to his wealth, or lack of it, he would be a very private man, but strangely, he did not hold back from giving her an insight into his finances, as he continued, 'To put your mind at rest, Brooke, apart from an inheritance from my father, my business yields sufficient for me to take a lovely English lady to dine, without it hurting my pocket.'

Warmed by his confidence and drowning in his charm, Brooke bit back a desire to know all about his work, all about his father, and his mother too. She turned her attention firmly to the menu. Any one of the questions she wanted to ask would show her interest, and that was something *she* could not afford. Somehow she had to get through this evening without giving him so much as a glimmer of how she felt about him.

She was still doing her best to show, outwardly, that she was unaffected by her escort, when the head waiter came and took their order. But it was a constant effort because, as if he had decided that nothing should mar her evening out, Jourdain was at his most pleasant.

Brooke attempted to take herself in hand when, shortly afterwards, they were conducted to a large baronial hall with the most massive open fireplace. Placed opposite him, she glanced around and saw that, of all the tables in the room, the one which had been reserved for Jourdain was situated in a discreet intimate corner.

She tried hard to concentrate on being a cool, calm dinner companion, but she soon discovered that even when sitting away from her across the table, Jourdain was as potent to her senses as ever.

In no time at all he had undone all her work to pull herself together. To begin with, when she knew he must be able to quote chapter and verse on the quality of various wines, he courteously asked if she had any preference. And, as soon as she had been drawn out by him, the conversation—how, she had no idea—suddenly centred on champagne. When Brooke confessed she had never tasted pink champagne, it was pink champagne he ordered.

She had a moment's respite from the headiness of him, when their first course arrived. He was an entertaining companion and she was amused many times by comments he made. She saw from his eyes that he in turn was amused by some of her replies. But, by the time the second course came, and then the third, Brooke was aware that all her attempts at resistance were collapsing.

The first course had been a small appetiser placed in

the middle of a large dinner plate. The second course, some sort of fish medallions in a wine sauce, had been served on the same-sized plate. For the third course, meat arrived with just the merest suggestion of vegetables. Because of this and the fact that they had lingered over each stage of the meal, Brook found she still had a little appetite for the next. In France, she had learned, cheese was eaten before dessert was reached.

She was cutting into a piece of cheese when suddenly she could not see why she should not give in to the pleasure of the evening. Quite simply any resistance she had left collapsed totally.

They had conversed on every subject under the sun save their two selves, but she found she could hold back nothing when, all at once, Jourdain asked,

'So, your father has his promotion, and has taken the first step to a life outside the home, and the twins will soon be settled at university.' Brooke had no wish by this time to sound a sour note by interrupting him to remind him that she was still having problems with Stephanie. 'Which leaves you,' he smiled. 'How about you, Brooke?'

'Oh, I've thought about me,' she replied. 'I've enrolled to start secretarial training next month.' She would have returned his smile—only it had gone.

'You hanker to be a career woman?' he asked, serious all at once.

'I don't know that it's a hankering so much as an inner feeling that I should be using my brain for something more than keeping house. Don't get me wrong,' her tongue started to run away with her, 'I love my home. I love home-making too. It gives me a good feeling when everything is going smoothly. It's just—I feel I should be doing something more worthwhile.'

'*Mon dieu!*' Jourdain erupted mildly. 'Can there be anything more worthwhile than being the home-maker for a family?' and when she had no reply to make, 'So your future plan is to be a secretary.' He paused, then, his eyes steady on her, and asked quietly, 'Is there any space for marriage in your future plan?'

Abruptly Brooke's eyes went down to her plate. She had not got around to thinking of marriage, but she knew that the only man she would want to marry was the man sitting straight opposite her, quietly waiting for her answer. A flurry of panic beset her, and she felt a need to let him know, lest she had given herself away, that he meant nothing to her. She gave herself no time to think further, and, her mouth curving upwards, she told him brightly,

'There's no one that special on my horizon at the moment.'

Jourdain smiled quietly, and nothing was said while the waiter came and exchanged their cheese plates for large dessert plates. As Brooke's panic died she wondered about that quiet smile. Suddenly she remembered how she had told him that there was some man in England she wanted to get back to. She knew then what that quiet smile meant—Jourdain knew she had lied to him on that occasion.

'So,' she said, dipping her spoon into her sweet with all the nonchalance of which she was capable, 'I'm a fibber.' On looking up she saw from his broad grin that he was more amused than annoyed. 'I was thinking of my father's welfare, and of my brother, when I said—er— you know.'

'Without too much assistance,' Jourdain opined, 'I have a feeling you could be something of a torment to a man.'

'*Moi!*' exclaimed Brooke, making an astounded face. Perhaps the champagne had gone to her head, or perhaps it was the effect Jourdain had on her, but she laughed, and told him happily, 'You say the nicest things, *monsieur*.'

That he should laugh too, pleased her. As did the way he left the subject of her and her family and spoke of other matters.

But what pleased her most of all was when the waiter came to Jourdain, and she caught the word *café*. She saw him glance towards another room where other diners had gone to take their coffee, and shake his head. She might be living in a dream world, but it seemed to her that on being asked where they would like to have their coffee—rather than join other diners and so ruin the rapport which she felt was flowing between them—Jourdain had instructed that coffee should be brought to the table.

Whether she was imagining it all, Brooke had no way of knowing, but they did take their coffee where they sat. It was then she realised, with the most romantic evening of her life almost over, that although they had talked and talked, and Jourdain had learned a little about her, she had learned nothing about him. She looked for a way to get him to talk about himself, and thought she had found it when she told him, truthfully,

'Nice as this château is, I think I prefer yours.'

'That—pleases me, Brooke,' he replied, and seemed so sincere, she was emboldened to press on.

'It's in excellent condition too.'

'It is important to me it should be so,' he replied. 'Château Marchais has been in the family for generations. It must be preserved for my children.'

'You have—children!'

'Not yet,' he smiled at her startled expression. 'First,' he said, his grey eyes holding hers, 'I must find myself a wife.'

Jealousy plunged a knife into her, but she managed to

hold herself in one piece, to enquire, 'You *want* to marry?'

'There is no other way for me,' he replied, a strange sort of tension suddenly about him. But it was so soon gone that Brooke knew she had imagined it, for his voice was easy, when he tacked on, 'My children must have my name.'

Brooke coped with her jealousy as best she could, but she sorely wished then that she had not got him on to this topic of conversation. Jourdain had done with the subject anyway, it seemed, for, when he spoke again, it was on more lighthearted matters and her jealousy was soon forgotten.

She wanted the evening to go on for ever but she knew it was over when Jourdain paid the bill and asked softly, 'You have enjoyed the evening, Brooke?'

How could she deny it? She guessed it was there on her face anyway. 'Yes,' she confessed.

Very little passed between them on the way back to the château. When the clock on the dash suddenly registered on her, Brooke broke the companionable silence to exclaim, not believing they had been away from the château for so long,

'It's past midnight!'

'The time has flown,' Jourdain agreed, and seemed quite content.

The magic of the evening was still with her as Jourdain escorted her inside the château. She half expected they would go up the stairs together, to part at her door, when he would move on to his room. But at the bottom of the stairs he halted, and she knew it would be there that she would thank him for the most wonderful evening of her life.

She turned, wanting to give him a modified version of how she felt, but her heart set off such a thunderous drumming at the tender look in his warm grey eyes that the words locked in her throat. She felt the warm clasp of his hand when he took hold of hers and was helpless to say anything at all when, solemnly, sincerely, he breathed,

'I should dearly like to kiss you, *chérie*, but I fear you will misunderstand.' He raised her hand to his lips, gently placed a kiss in her palm, and folded her fingers over it. *'Bonne nuit, ma mie,'* he said softly.

Her hand clenched tight on his kiss, *'Bonne nuit,* Jourdain,' Brooke managed to whisper, and as he turned abruptly about and strode off down the hall, she went up the stairs.

When she awoke the next morning, Brooke did not get up immediately. The coming of daylight in no way detracted from her pleasure in reliving the joy the previous evening had been to her, just as she had on going to bed.

Again she dwelt on how quickly the hours had gone by. Had they really taken all that time to eat their meal? Jourdain had agreed that the time had flown for him too—was it possible that he had been as enthralled as she?

Logic tried to edge out her fantasies. Logic which said that with a charm as natural as his, it had called for no great effort on his part to ensure that she enjoyed the evening to the full. But she did not want to listen to logic. She was in love, and Jourdain had wanted to kiss her ...

She recalled how he had not kissed her for fear she might misunderstand, and suddenly, logic was starting to take over from her dreamy mood. For several minutes Brooke did not know where she was. Then, all at once, the most appalling thought struck.

Jourdain had said he had to marry, but, since she could

not figure anywhere in his marriage plans, had he been
trying to tell her that any kiss they shared would lead
precisely nowhere? Had he seen how much she cared for
him? she wondered, starting to panic. Had his 'I fear you
will misunderstand' been merely his way of saying that in
other circumstances he would end such a pleasant
evening with a kiss? But, because he had seen the love
she had for him, because of her inexperience in the art of
light dalliance, he feared she might misunderstand and,
bearing in mind how his other kisses had got out of hand,
believe that whatever happened after that kiss was a
declaration of love!

Her palms started to sweat, and Brooke owned that she
had been open to seduction. She had been so enchanted
by him, and by the evening, that she knew she would not
have stood a chance had he kissed her and wanted more
than one kiss.

Thoughts of how vulnerable she had been had her
hopping out of bed and hurrying to get washed and
dressed. Not that she was going downstairs. Jourdain
must have known she was his for the taking. She never
wanted to have to face him again. But, unable to live with
her thoughts, she had to do something.

Well aware that she was not ready to see anybody just
yet, at the same time Brooke could not stay in her room to
be bombarded by fresh, unwanted, pride-destroying
thoughts. Stephanie's room was the obvious choice.

Agitation kept stride with her as Brooke dashed the
short distance along the landing, frantic to think up some
way to show Jourdain he had got it all wrong if he
thought she cared so much as a button for him. She
opened Stephanie's door in a panic—then, at the sight
that met her eyes, she had something else to panic about.
Not only was Stephanie up and dressed, but her
wardrobe doors were wide open, and she was throwing

the contents into a couple of open suitcases on the bed.

'What are you doing.' exclaimed Brooke, able to see quite clearly what her sister was doing, but unable to adjust so soon from one trauma to another one.

'What does it look as if I'm doing?' Stephanie snapped sourly. 'I'm going home.'

'But—but . . .'

'But nothing,' Stephanie interrupted tartly. 'If you think I'm going to stick around here now I've been made a fool of, you have another think coming!'

Winded for the second time that morning, Brooke got it all together as Stephanie scurried back and forth to the wardrobes.

'You're—referring to the fact that—J-Jourdain took me out to dinner last night?' she got out.

'And *other* things,' Stephanie tossed at her. 'He's never taken *me* out to dinner—not without Mélisande and her mother being there too, anyway.'

Brooke knew then that there was no sense in love. Because even though all she wanted was to get Stephanie away from the château; even though she thought she never wanted to look Jourdain in the face again, she experienced the most desperate longing to stay.

But she had to turn her back on what she wanted, not on Stephanie. Years of caring for her sister made it second nature for her to push aside her own trauma to ask,

'You don't think maybe we should have a word with Doctor Delage to see if you're fit to travel?'

'Stuff the doctor,' said Stephanie rudely. 'I'm travelling.'

From where Brooke was standing, she could see no mark of ill health on her, and could only hope, with Stephanie determined to leave, that this latest emotional upset would not bring about another attack of asthma.

'I'll go and get my things together,' she said quietly, and was at the door when she turned back to state, 'one of us will have to tell Jourdain we're leaving,' and because she still didn't know how she was going to face him, 'Will you . . .' she began, when Stephanie cut in,

'There's no need for either of us to tell him anything. He's not here.'

'Not here?' Surprise took Brooke a few steps back into the room. 'What do you mean—he's not here?'

'Didn't he tell you, while he was busily wining and dining you last night,' Stephanie inserted sarcastically, 'about his business meeting in Paris first thing this morning?' Dumbly Brooke shook her head, and heard that it was Mélisande who had imparted this piece of news to her sister. 'According to Mélisande,' Stephanie continued airily, 'Jourdain would have to get off at first light to make it in time.'

Logic told Brooke she should be grateful not to have to see him again. But it was with a very heavy heart that, with Stephanie in the passenger seat of the car, she left the château shortly afterwards.

Courtesy had demanded that she did not leave without some show of appreciation, but the non-flowery thank-you note she had penned thanking Jourdain for his hospitality had been kept to the minimum of words.

Mélisande had been quite bewildered to learn they were leaving when Brooke handed the note over into her keeping. She had assumed that it was on account of Stephanie's illness that they had to go, and, although Brooke had taken to the young French woman, she let her carry on with that assumption.

Brooke expected Stephanie to remain in the same ill-tempered mood she had been in from the start that morning. They had been on the road for less than an hour, though, when Stephanie began to come out of her ourness. By the time they were on the ferry—it had to be admitted, after a longish wait—Stephanie was almost back to being the person she was when everything was going her way.

Perhaps it was just France, Brooke mused. Her own personality had undergone a change while she had been here. On reflection, though, she saw it was not so much that her own personality had undergone a change, as that without knowing it, she had fallen in love with Jourdain. That had been the reason she had been so at odds with herself.

She did not want to think about Jourdain, or her love for him. Instead she concentrated on Stephanie, and decided that maybe her sister's return to good humour was because, away from the château, she was seeing things in a clearer perspective.

At any rate, Brooke mused, as she watched a restless Stephanie move here, there and all over the place, her sister was looking more cheerful and, thank goodness, she was showing no sign of going into laboured breathing.

'Guess what?' Stephanie suddenly bounded back to come to sit opposite her.

'You tell me,' Brooke replied, noting an excitement in her sister's eyes which had nothing to do with illness.

'I've just met the dishiest feller—and—wait for it, he only happens to be in his final year at York, that's all!'

Softly, softly catchee monkey, Brooke thought, and tried to keep calm as she asked casually, 'Do I take it you've decided to go to university after all?'

'If you want to call me a spoiled little bitch, I'll let you,' Stephanie invited with a return of her old grin. 'But wild horses wouldn't keep me away if this guy's a sample of the talent up there!'

Brooke's calm momentarily deserted her. Her voice

was a shade waspish, she had to own, as she remarked, 'It didn't take you long to forget Jourdain Marchais, did it?'

'He was quite something, wasn't he?'

'Quite something!' exclaimed Brooke, astonished that her sister could be so lighthearted, when only a few days ago she had been ready to take her own life on account of him. 'I thought you were head over heels in love with him!'

'I *was* smitten,' Stephanie admitted. 'But with Jourdain treating me like a kid all the time, it finally got through to me last night, that I just wasn't going to get anywhere with him.'

'Where exactly were you hoping to "get" with him?' Brooke questioned, having suffered agonies on her sister's behalf, and not ready to let go, now she had got her talking.

'It's academic,' Stephanie shrugged. 'He refused to play ball.'

Quite suddenly, Brooke saw through Stephanie's façade of being lighthearted, but, needing her trust if she was to help her, it was gently that she told her,

'It won't wash, chick. No girl attempts suicide just because . . .'

'*Suicide*? What in creation are you talking about?'

'Don't try to deny it, love,' Brooke tried to soothe. Ignoring the fact that Stephanie was staring at her as though she had taken leave of her senses, she went on, 'I was there. You can't have forgotten how I jumped into the river after you to get you out. You tried to . . .'

'Good—God!' gasped Stephanie, her expression utterly incredulous. 'I thought you'd landed in the river the same way I did!' she exclaimed, flabbergasted. But she rapidly transferred her incredulity to Brooke, as she recounted, 'If you remember, it had been raining cats and dogs pretty well non-stop for forty-eight hours.

When I took a sprint along the river bank that afternoon it was pretty slippery. I heard a sound behind me, thought it was Jourdain coming after me, and put my anchors on fast. The only trouble was,' she added ruefully, 'that I'd managed to choose the muddiest, most slippery part in which to skid to a halt. You *must* have heard my banshee-like wail of horror when I lost my balance and knew I couldn't avoid taking a header?'

Shaken rigid, Brooke stared at her in disbelief. Yes, she'd heard her sister cry out, but she had thought it a cry of anguish—which was what it had been, but not for the reasons she had thought.

'You . . .' Brooke started to surface, 'you—went into the river—accidentally?'

'Of course I did. I thought, when you splashed in to join me, that you'd found the same muddy patch as I had. Good grief, Brooke!' Stephanie exclaimed, shocked as it dawned on her what her elder sister had thought. 'I know I was in a bit of a state. And who wouldn't be,' she defended, 'after seeing you in a clinch with the man I hadn't been able to get to first base with? But, good heavens, I love life too much to ever consider doing such a terrible thing!'

Brooke felt indeseribably relieved Stephanie was as emotionally stable as she ever could be with her temperament. But with Jourdain never far from Brooke's mind, close on the heels of that relief, came the memory of how callous she had thought him at the time. She had taken a swing at him precisely because of his callousness, and he had been astonished, she remembered. She was remembering too how astounded he had looked when she had told him that Stephanie had attempted to drown herself. Later, he had asked if she had been out since 'your sister "fell" into the river'. Brooke knew then that the only reason for his astonishment was that he knew, as he had known all along, that Stephanie had never attempted to take her life.

Still shaken, Brooke felt uncertainty about the clarity of her thoughts. She still had to be clear about one thing.

'Jourdain,' she said, 'he knew you hadn't attempted to drown yourself?'

'Of course he knew,' Stephanie confirmed promptly. 'It never occurred to him that my fall into the river was anything but the accident it was,' she added stoutly, and continued, 'I know that for a fact, because after he'd sent you to get changed and he'd calmed me down from the hysterics I was having because—to top everything—I knew I must look like a drowned rat, he apologised for not having noticed that the river path needed to have some gravel put down. He must have seen my skid marks. He must have thought you'd skidded too,' she concluded.

Remembering how she had seen new gravel on that river path only yesterday, not only endorsed the fact that Jourdain did not take his responsibilities lightly, but also backed up what Stephanie had just said. By now Brooke felt her emotions were in so much of a jumble, she no longer knew whether she loved or hated him.

'He—thought we were a couple of English eccentrics out for a fully-clothed dip,' she mumbled out loud.

'You didn't tell him you thought I'd had a go at "ending it all", did you?'

'I did,' Brooke admitted, 'and hit him for what I considered his callous attitude.'

'You *hit* him!' Stephanie exclaimed on a hushed breath. 'My God, Brooke, you chanced your arm! He'd want retribution for that. Oh dear,' she exclaimed suddenly, 'it all fits into place!'

'What does?' asked Brooke, suddenly at a total loss.

'You're not going to like this,' Stephanie warned, 'but

since it seems to be confession time, I'd better tell you that I—well, to start at the beginning.'

'I wish you would,' Brooke said sternly. She felt all over the place as it was without Stephanie stringing it out for dramatic effect.

Stephanie was looking more sheepish than dramatic. As though she wanted it all said and done, she revealed how apart from not liking Brooke very much just then, she had blamed her, not only for being the indirect cause of her soaking, but also for Jourdain seeing her without a curl to her name. She had felt fine, though, once Madame Lasserre had tucked her up in bed. Later Jourdain had come to see her and told her that Brooke was determined to take her back to England the next day.

'He wouldn't care for you being bossy either, Brooke,' Stephanie paused to insert, and went on, 'I told him I wasn't leaving—no way. But Jourdain said that, as my elder sister was acting in my father's stead, he would have to comply with father's wishes and see to it that I went with you. That was—big hint—unless as a result of my soaking, I caught a chill which would make it impossible for you to take me back to England.'

This was the first she'd heard of Jourdain accepting her as her father's envoy, and it took Brooke's breath away. She tried to clear away more of the fog. 'But instead of some fictitious chill, you had a genuine attack of asthma.'

Stephanie looked sheepish again. 'There was nothing genuine about that attack,' she confessed. 'Don't hate me too much, Brooke,' she hurried on. 'I know I was a pain, and I behaved like a spoiled brat to you, but I wasn't ill at all.'

'B-but . . .' Brooke just could not believe it even when Stephanie said,

'If anyone should know how to fake asthma, I should.'

'But what about Matthieu Delage? He gave you some tablets. He . . .'

'Placebos, most likely. He knew I was faking anyway, when he took my ever-so-normal pulse. Just as Jourdain knew when I tipped him the wink before the doctor arrived.' Stephanie raced on, 'Anyway, I knew the doctor was on to me when the wrong sound came back when he tapped my chest. When he took out his stethoscope ready to sound my lungs and there wasn't a thing wrong with them, I had to think fast. I told him I was going through an emotional crisis with which I didn't want to worry you. I also told him of my history of asthma—so he decided to keep an eye on me.'

If there were any more shocks in store for her, then Brooke did not want to know. There were limits, she discovered, and she had just reached hers.

'You want boiling in oil,' she told Stephanie icily. 'Along with Jourdain Marchais and Matthieu Delage,' she threw in for good measure, since he of all of them should have told her there was nothing wrong with her sister.

'I agree,' said Stephanie contritely. 'In my defence, though, I didn't see then that it wasn't me but you Jourdain didn't want to leave.'

'And why,' Brooke questioned, still icily, 'should he want me to stay? I'd told him in no uncertain terms that I couldn't wait to leave.'

'My giddy aunt, Brooke, you're so dim where men like him are concerned!' her younger sister informed her. 'Here we have a man who, by the very nature of his taking on not one job but two, shows he dearly loves a challenge, and what do you do? You hit him! Not content with that, you offend his house and insult his hospitality by saying you can't wait to be shot of it. And it surprises you when he decides to make you hang around to eat your words? Did he have a few scores to settle with you! Why,' she exclaimed, 'taking you out to dinner last night must only have been a warm up! Really, Brooke, I didn't get you out of there a moment too soon!'

At any other time Brooke, who had been the one to want Stephanie away from the château, might have seen her sister's remarks as comical. Not then, though. There was too much pain inside for her to find anything remotely funny in what Stephanie said.

Their father was pleased to see them, and accepted without question Stephanie's, 'I got homesick,' as a reason for cutting short her stay. Brooke went to bed that night only for thoughts of Jourdain to keep her awake.

He was still refusing to be ejected from her thoughts when she got up the next morning. Away from France, away from him, memories intruded as she cooked her father's breakfast.

'It's good to have you back, Brooke,' Alec Farringdon said when she placed a plate of bacon and egg in front of him. 'Aren't you having any?' he enquired, when she sat down with nothing but a cup of coffee in front of her.

Brooke reckoned she was off bacon and egg for life. 'I'll have something with Stephanie when she gets up,' she replied. She saw him off to work, then went to round up the soiled laundry, with Jourdain in her head again.

Whether he had wanted retribution for all the times she had offended him, or whether he didn't, retribution was his. She had fallen in love with him—he had seen that love—and had walked away. Pride told her to hate him. But love, she had discovered, was stronger than pride.

By eleven that morning, Stephanie had surfaced and was all for going round to see 'the gang'. When requested to bring down any dirty washing she had unpacked, although impatient to be off, she replied,

'Actually, I haven't unpacked yet. But after the lovely clothes you made me while I was away, who could deny you anything?'

She hurried up the stairs, to be back down again in fifteen minutes, her arms loaded with what seemed to be everything she had taken with her, all of which could do with 'a rinse through'. 'I'd stay and help, but I'd only be in the way,' she said, and was halfway to the door when she turned to grin, 'Er—to save yourself a heart attack— don't look in my room, it's a tip!' Then, pure Stephanie, she said 'I love you, flower.'

Brooke had hardly closed the door when the telephone rang. Certain the call would be for Stephanie, who had spent half of the previous evening on the phone letting her friends know she was back, she went and picked it up. Then she very nearly dropped it.

'Brooke?' enquired a very faintly accented voice. A voice she would know anywhere.

CHAPTER NINE

BROOKE swallowed hard, her knees about to buckle. Why was Jourdain ringing her home? She clung to the sudden hope that maybe he had not seen her love for him, and that pride would help her to mask it.

'Yes, this is Brooke,' she replied coolly.

'Your voice sounds as stiff as the—bread-and-butter letter I've just walked in to find,' Jourdain remarked, an inflection in his voice telling her he cared neither for her way of talking or writing.

The fact that he had wasted no time phoning to chide her for the way she had written passed her by, so great was the effort she was making to keep cool.

'What makes you think I should sound any different?' she asked with a touch of haughtiness to help her out.

There was a moment or two of silence during which she knew she should replace the receiver, but found that her hand and arm would not obey the instruction from her brain. Then Jourdain, with a warmth that almost fractured her, started to reply,

'I thought, after the—enjoyment—we shared on Sunday evening when . . .'

'Actually, *monsieur*,' she cut in, 'I'm not remotely interested in remembering that evening.' His cruelty in not hesitating to remind her of the evening that she had thought so wonderful was all she needed. In the next instant her paralysed hand and arm found release, and before she could have second thoughts, the receiver was back on its cradle,.

For the next ten minutes Brooke damned Jourda[i]
Marchais for still getting to her, even with the Chann[e]
dividing them. Something wet on her cheek made h[e]
realise that she was crying. Furiously she wiped her tea[r]
away and cursed him some more that just because t[he]
aristocratic swine had not liked her 'thank you for n[y]
bread and butter' letter, he should ring her to take her [to]
task about it.

Damn him, she thought again, as she loaded t[he]
washing machine. The calm person she had been seem[ed]
gone for ever as she took herself off to the shops with t[he]
intention of replenishing the larder, only to return hom[e]
and find she had forgotten half the items she had go[ne]
out for.

Hunger brought Stephanie dashing home to grab a bi[te]
around lunchtime, but she had no sooner eaten, than sh[e]
was off again with a, 'I'll tidy my room before I go [to]
bed—promise!'

At two o'clock, her heart not really in it, but with som[e]
of the washing dry enough for ironing, Brooke set up t[he]
ironing board. At five past two the door bell wen[t]
Automatically she switched off the iron and went [to]
answer the door—and almost fainted on the spot!

'Your way of speaking to me over the phone is mo[st]
aggravating', said Jourdain Marchais, looking taller an[d]
more good-looking than ever, and as calculated now [to]
ruin her peace of mind as he had been all day.

Her heart on a merry-go-round, Brooke took a[n]
unthought-out, utterly staggered step backwards. To[o]
late she saw that Jourdain had accepted her moveme[nt]
back from the door as an invitation to cross t[he]
threshhold.

It was also too late then to obey the logic whic[h]
belatedly told her she should have closed the door o[n]

im. Her innate good manners surfaced to help her out,
nd she led the way into the sitting room, her thoughts
oing off at a tangent.

'Can I offer you some refreshment?' she asked, her
oice coolly civilised in her determination to show that
ny idea he might have that she was in love with him,
as completely false.

'I have more important things on my mind than to
ant to sit—*politely* drinking tea,' he stressed, as if her
ttempt at good manners grated on him.

His tone was tough. His look was tough. There was
lso a certain tiredness around his eyes that suggested he
ad worked hard during the last twenty-four hours. To
rooke's mind, though, those lines of tiredness could just
s easily have been the result of playing hard.

'They must be important indeed.' Jealousy at that last
hought brought a trace of acid to her cool voice. 'You
aven't had time to get here by ferry.'

'There's an air-strip not far from here,' Jourdain tossed
a as though it were by the way, leaving her to guess if he
ad chartered a plane or had been at the controls of his
wn light aircraft. Either way she was shaken.

'Your—errand must have been truly urgent,' she made
erself reply. Hurt dug away at her, and more acid came
o her tongue. 'Surely you haven't raced here merely
ecause you don't like my way of speaking to you over
he phone?'

Clearly he did not like her attitude. The sudden jut of
is jaw told her so; and that was before he bit
ggressively, 'I need a few answers from you, Brooke
arringdon. It was not in my mind to repeat my
elephone call, only to have you put the phone down on
ne again before I had a chance to get started.'

'I see,' she replied, playing for time, because she saw

absolutely nothing. Then, with a sudden feeling that he
would trample all over her if she let him, her weakened
backbone found some stiffening. 'No doubt one of your
questions was an enquiry into my sister's health since she
has been away from your home and the good offices of
Doctor Delage.' Her voice was suddenly tart, when she
rammed home, 'Stephanie, *monsieur*, is in perfec
health—as she has been all along.'

'Ah!' said Jourdain, any small sign of surprise quickly
gone, a glint appearing in those grey eyes that refused to
look away from her. 'Stephanie has confessed that she
was never ill?'

'Stephanie,' Brooke told him coldly, 'has confessed
that it never occurred to her to *pretend* to be ill, until you
put the suggestion to her.'

'Mmm,' came from Jourdain, his look thoughtful. He
gave a resigned shrug of his broad shoulders which,
oddly, at the same time, appeared to square them. Then
quietly, his watchful eyes upon hers, he said, 'It would
seem, Brooke, that before I can come to the point of why
I am here, you require an explanation. It—may take
some time, you will be more comfortable sitting down,
n'est-ce pas?'

She had no intention of sitting down, preferring to
remain standing, so that he would go the sooner. But her
intention somehow got lost when he stretched out a hand
and took hold of her arm. At his electric touch Brooke
moved away, and was promptly so scared he would read
exactly what his touch could do to her that she was forced
to follow the action through and make believe her
movement had been towards the settee.

Her insides like so much jelly, it was more disconcert-
ing than ever to have Jourdain come and sit down beside
her. When he half turned so he could look into her face

he had a dreadful time trying to remember what they had been talking about.

'There—is no need for you to explain anything, *monsieur*,' she told him cuttingly, her memory block suddenly cleared. 'Stephanie has explained everything quite adequately, I assure you.'

The glint was back in his eyes, but if he did not like it that she insisted on calling him *monsieur*, he did not take her to task about it, as on one other occasion she could remember. Instead he did himself no favour and said, his voice quite still,

'I believe my explanation will vary greatly from that of your sister.'

'Don't you dare call my sister a liar!' Brooke forgot her cool to defend her. Jourdain's raised right eyebrow was instrumental in reminding her that Stephanie's asthma attack had been one great whopping lie, but Brooke would not back down. To his credit, Jourdain did not argue the point.

'I would not dream of being so ungallant,' he murmured. 'Although I think you will have to agree that Stephanie has the capacity to—dramatise—the truth a little.'

'I'm now aware that she faked being ill,' Brooke stated flatly, her calm outwardly restored.

'I was not referring to her pretended illness,' Jourdain said quietly, 'but to the fact that she missed her father more than she realised, and that I was the only male adult around. This all began when Stephanie wrote to you embellishing the liking she had for me into a love she did not truly feel in any way.'

'She . . .' Brooke started, but her loyalty to Stephanie was countered by the truth of what Jourdain had said. Her three years of illness, and the fact that we babied her for so long, has made her a little immature for her years,' was the best she could do in Stephanie's defence.

'Of course,' he agreed, and for a moment, with his opinion so at one with hers, Brooke forgot to oppose him when he added, 'university will see her catching up fast, I am sure. But,' he went on, quick to note she had no argument, and intent, while she was still agreeing with him, on progressing further, 'your sister was no problem while Eléanore, my sister, was there.'

'She became a problem—when your sister had to go away?' asked Brooke, somewhat startled, because her memory of his attitude was that he hadn't cared a damn.

'Not so much a problem,' he admitted, 'but, *naturellement*, I had to consider sending her back to England when Eléanore hurried to her husband's bedside.'

'But you . . .' gasped Brooke.

Jourdain's mouth, for the first time, quirked into that smile which she found quite devastating and only then realised she had missed. 'Your phone call caught me at a wrong moment,' he confessed. 'As you love your family, so I love mine. I was much concerned over Henri, and thought it more important to assure Eléanore—who had enough anxiety over her husband—that Stephanie was no problem. I had just finished telling Eléanore over the telephone that I would see Stephanie was not bored, and had promised I would find her some occupation in my study, when your call came from England.

'You were charming, at first,' slipped out before Brooke could stop it, and her heart missed a panicky beat when, with an alert look in his eyes, Jourdain said slowly, 'Even in stress, one tries to be polite.'

Oh dear, she thought, remembering his comment on her politeness earlier. Did he know she felt full of stress inside—for all she was trying desperately to hide it?

'Well, your charm didn't last long, did it?' she challenged, her voice a snappy reaction to the thought that Jourdain seemed to know precisely just how soft she was inside about him.

'It didn't have much of a chance,' he agreed. 'There was I, doing my best to be civil, while all the time your voice was growing cooler and cooler, when, as far as I knew, I had done nothing wrong. I did not like it, Brooke,' he admitted honestly, 'that some frigid-sounding Englishwoman whom I had never met should question my morality, or make my decisions for me when, had you left things alone, I would most likely have contacted your father to suggest Stephanie finish her stay in my home at some other time.'

'You put the phone down on me,' Brooke remembered, to let him know that her putting the phone down on him had only evened up the score.

'I'd had enough of you trying to give me orders,' he owned. 'Yet for the next twenty-four hours you continued to annoy me. Not another moment's thought should I have given you, yet you and that call continued to plague me, until, suddenly, there you were.'

'You—er—didn't expect me to take you up on your suggestion that I should come and get Stephanie?' she asked, his quirky smile threatening her calm again.

'I don't think I did,' he conceded. 'But if to see you there in my forecourt was something of a surprise, it was as nothing to the other surprises you had for me.'

'You're referring to my telling you about Stephanie's infatuation for you?'

'Mon Dieu!' Jourdain exclaimed softly, 'did you have some surprises for me that night! Though perhaps,' he added on reflection, 'total amazement at your cool, colossal impertinence was more what I experienced.'

Brooke remembered that night well. She would never forget it. 'You—er—didn't like it when I asked you if you—were—er . . .'

'Trifling, was the word you used,' he reminded her. By the sound of it, he had forgotten nothing that had been said that night. 'At first,' he went on, 'I just could not believe my hearing. That you, as outwardly frigid as I had supposed, should sit as a guest in my *salon*, and, careless of the insolence, *dare* to ask if I was trifling with the young adult who for a short while had been entrusted to my safe keeping—all this had me positively astounded.'

'I had to know,' said Brooke faintly.

'Did you also have to add injury to the insult, by casting aspersions on my honour as a gentleman?' he enquired mildly.

More than a little uncomfortable to be so taken to task, however gently, Brooke suddenly woke up to the fact that for the last few minutes she had lost all sight of being obstructive. Damn it, she roused herself, who did he think he was that he should have her wriggling on the end of a pin? It was high time she asserted herself.

'Was it gentlemanly,' she came out fighting, 'when you've just said you were considering sending Stephanie home, to give me all that verbiage about being unable to do so because you couldn't break your word to my father?'

She could see, by his stern expression, that Jourdain did not like her changed attitude. Oddly, he did not get aggressive in return, but, in a mild voice with even a trace of admiration in his eyes, he stated quietly,

'I saw passion in you almost from the first, Brooke. I was . . .'

Not wanting to be reminded of her passion—in other

directions, she was quick to butt in, 'You also saw me as frigid! Is that why you suggested you'd—you'd . . .' her voice started to falter, but she made herself go on, '. . . you'd pretend to be enamoured of me? Not, as you said, to spur Stephanie's pride and make her want to leave voluntarily,' her voice picked up angry speed, 'but to pay me back; to pay back the frigid English miss for her insolence, by making her have forty fits at the thought she might have to go to bed with a man?'

Jourdain heard her out to the end of her tirade, then said quite simply, 'If I could deny it, Brooke, I would.' His hand shot out to grab a hold of hers when she made a jerky movement as if to leave the settee. He went on, his hand holding her there, 'But since I want no truth hidden or evaded from now on, I have to admit I am not a man who can take lightly an insult to my family name, or to my personal integrity. Had you been a man, I could have silenced you with a punch on the jaw. But you are a woman.'

'A frigid Englishwoman,' she snapped, hurt and unthinking, as she yanked her hand out of his grip.

'An *outwardly* frigid Englishwoman,' he corrected, 'but a woman with spirit enough to take on all comers where the wellbeing of those she loves is concerned. A woman who, for all her cool outward appearance, could not hide the passion in her eyes.' Brooke quelled her impulse to rush for the door, and he went on, his grey eyes fixed nowhere but on her. 'And, if I wanted another surprise, a woman with whom I very soon discovered I was not having to pretend to be—enamoured.'

'No!' said Brooke sharply. 'Oh, no! I'm not swallowing that.' Agitation, fear, a feeling of not knowing quite what to say or do, had her rushing out with the first thing that came into her head. 'I don't know what your p-purpose is in coming here, but if it's to . . . Well, in any case, I'm just not going to be made a—be made . . .'

Jourdain was gently soothing. 'Calm down, *petite*, I'm not going to harm you.' His words brought the sudden feeling that, if she could not control herself, and went headlong into another outburst then Jourdain would have no doubts about how eaily he could get to her.

She took a deep breath, and gathered up every wayward scrap of self-control. 'Tell me more,' she attempted acidly, and afraid her tongue might run away with her again, decided not to say another word.

'I should dearly like to kiss the vitriol away from your lips,' Jourdain murmured, which was of no great help to her self-control. He withstood one of her best withering glances, and returned to what he had been saying. 'It gave me some satisfaction, I admit, to make you forget yourself and reveal your true anger at such a suggestion. I'll even admit to feeling a certain smugness that night when you left the *salon* and went to your bed in a fury,' he added, bearing with the stony-faced expression she showed him. 'But even by the very next morning, my anticipation of more enjoyment at your expense was, to my surprise, obscured by a feeling of concern for you.'

Woodenly, Brooke looked at him. She had not liked it one little bit to hear him admit he had deliberately set her up. 'Concern?' she enquired sarcastically. '*You* surprise *me*!' She found that her heart refused to back up her stony front, and she weakened, to ask, albeit coolly, 'What brought about this lessening of your—enjoyment?'

'The weather,' he replied, without hesitation. 'I'd seen you setting off down the drive. The next time I looked out of the study window, the heavens had opened. In view of the antipathy I felt towards you, it should not have concerned me that you would get drenched, but my hand went to my car keys, and I was on my way to find you before I realised what I was doing.'

'I was already drenched when you came along,' she told him coldly, and, with memories of his amusement at the sight she had been, she did not thank him for his 'concern'. 'It didn't take you long to remember your "enjoyment" at my expense, did it?' she challenged. 'In no time at all, you were talking again of being prepared to "honour" your outrageous suggestion.'

'You are right to be angry,' Jourdain told her, 'but in my defence, I discovered that you could get me annoyed with the most aggravating ease.' He went on quickly when her expression showed, that excuse had not gone down well, 'In the car I experienced a momentary sympathy for you and I just did not want to fight with you. Before that sympathy could linger, the next second you had again succeeded in stirring my anger, by suggesting that I might make capital of my new knowledge of your sister's infatuation for me.'

'I couldn't speak without offending you in some way or other,' Brooke snapped tartly.

'So it seemed, initially,' he agreed. Then his quirky smile was there again, and, all at once, a warmer note had crept into his voice. 'You were not talking, but silent and asleep, the next time I saw you.'

'If you're going to refer to that time when you crept up on me and kissed me——' Brooke cut in, remembering in agitation how she had responded, only Jourdain would not let her stop him.

'I have to refer to it,' he said. 'For that was the second time I found myself acting without knowing what motivated me. I came into that room, saw you asleep, beautiful, and without knowing what had come over me,

I had to kiss you.'

For all of two seconds Brooke was stumped. The notion teased her that Jourdain was trying to tell her something more. But then common sense jumped in to tell her to ignore all such vague ideas.

'I'll tell you what came over you,' she said quickly. 'It was nothing more than your basic instinct, the instinct of the flirt you are. Seeing an opportunity not to be missed, you took it.' There, she thought, that has set him straight.

When Jourdain did not immediately reply, she suddenly began to feel wary. A moment later, she knew she was right. For, after deliberating on her outburst for a few seconds, he said softly,

'We will leave for the moment, whether or not I am a flirt. But tell me, Brooke, since you are not a flirt, why did you respond as you did to my kiss?'

'I—I . . .' She felt hot all over. 'I was—half asleep,' she said, and hastily changed the subject. 'Anyway, if it hadn't been for that—that—for Stephanie seeing us, she would never have raced off the way she did. She would never have . . .'

'Fallen in the water,' Jourdain let her get away with it.

'Yes, *fallen*,' said Brooke crisply. 'You knew that,' she accused, and warmed to her theme. 'All the time I was telling you she'd attempted suicide, you knew she'd slipped and not jumped. When I was worried sick . . .'

'I should go down on my knees and apologise for that,' he butted in gently. 'But the truth is, Brooke, things were happening inside me, and happening so fast. It is no wonder to me now that I lost my sense of perspective.'

'What—kind—of things?' she questioned slowly.

'You,' he said simply. 'When I caught sight of you flying through the air to join Stephanie in the river, and saw from the marks on the bank how the accident had occurred, I knew only that, whatever happened to Stephanie, first I must get you out.'

'You got Stephanie out first,' Brooke reminded him bluntly. 'As I remember it, I got myself out.'

'She was nearer to the bank,' he explained. 'As I got myself together a quick check showed me you were in no danger. Then with Stephanie having hysterics and the river bank a quagmire, logic told me that I should get you away from there before you went in again. The quickest way to do that was to carry your sister indoors. I knew you would follow.'

Brooke digested what he had said. On edge because of the growing feeling that he was playing another of his games in order to send her up, she asked acidly,

'Did your logic tell you it might be good sport to hint to Stephanie that she might suffer a chill from her experience?'

'*Non!*' Jourdain denied sharply, but semi-retracted that '*non*' to admit openly, 'Not then. That came later. I left Madame Lasserre in attendance on Stephanie, and went to my study.' He paused, and then, his eyes attentively on hers, told her, 'But I could not start on my work. You see, Brooke, my head was full of you.'

'Of me? Not Stephanie?' She had asked the question before common sense told her Jourdain must be hell bent on leading her on for some obscure reason of his own.

'Of you, Brooke,' he confirmed solemnly. 'There you were, this outwardly cool and controlled Englishwoman—and yet nowhere near as cool as you tried to pretend. There was passion in you, I knew it. Before I kissed you, I knew it. I had seen that passion again, only a short while before, when to my astonishment, you hit me in a fury. I had just faced the fact that I was becoming more and more intrigued by you, when, suddenly, there you were in my study with me.'

Her heart gave a giddy flip to hear that he had been intrigued by her, but she remained outwardly composed to retort, 'Was this intrigue the reason for your hint to Stephanie that she should feign illness? It had nothing to do with the fact, of course, that I'd offended your hospitality by telling you I couldn't wait to leave.'

'It had nothing at all to do with my being offended,' Jourdain told her, his expression serious. 'Nor did I immediately think of bringing Stephanie into my schemes. Even then I did not have the answer to why it was so important to me that you should not leave my home. All I knew was that there was something alive in me that wanted to know more of you.' Brooke's heart gave another giddy lurch. 'In the hope that, if I got you alone over dinner, you might change your mind about leaving,' he went on, 'I told Madame Lasserre to advise your sister that she must rest for the remainder of the day, and that dinner would be brought to her room.'

The picture, or at least some of it, was becoming clearer. 'Your plan to get me to change my mind came unstuck, when I didn't join you for dinner that night?'

'It did,' he nodded, 'and that made me angry, although I still did not know why then. But it made me more determined than ever that you should stay.'

His plotting seemed less obscure then, but Brooke still didn't like the fact that she had been at the butt end of his schemes. 'How lucky for you,' she told him icily, 'that Stephanie went along with you, and played her role so well.'

'Lucky!' he exclaimed. 'You think I had any luck in my scheming to have some time alone with you! You were so busy nursing your sister, I never saw you! *Mon Dieu!*

Matthieu Delage was making more progress with you than I!'

'Progress!' sprang from Brooke, her heart a fevered engine of activity. That was until she got it all together. 'Goodness' she burst out then. 'You're a worse flirt than he is!' She saw it all then, and words were tumbling from her lips unchecked, twin patches of angry colour in her cheeks as she forgot to be cool, and raged, 'All you wanted, with your talk of being intrigued by me, was a flirtation. It niggled away at your masculine pride, didn't it, when I wouldn't . . .' More colour came to her face as she remembered how she nearly had. 'Well,' she charged on, 'if you've come to my home only to try to absolve your masculine pride, hard luck! I'm no more interested in a flirtation with you now than I was then!' At that point Brooke ran out of steam.

'Have you quite finished?' Jourdain enquired in the most courteous of terms, cool in contrast to her fire.

'Quite,' she retorted stiffly.

'Then perhaps I may be allowed to tell you that it was never in my mind to have a flirtation with you.'

His comment, with its suggestion that he had never found her in the least desirable, almost sank her. But it was only for a moment, more memories had crowded in.

'No?' she jibed. 'You'll be telling me next that I imagined it, and that you never even kissed me.'

'Oh, I kissed you, Brooke, and you responded,' he said, when she would rather he had not. 'But I did not kiss you for any motive other that the fact the I could not help myself. Which makes me wonder,' he went on, his eyes on her face, 'since you have stated that you were not interested in a flirtation either, if you responded for the same reason. That you too could not help yourself.'

Her agitation was instant. Soon, if she did not stop

him, he would have confirmation that she loved him. But, she could not allow that.

It was not easy, with such agitation stabbing at her, to appear as casual as he was. But Brooke thought she had managed it. Her air was that of someone more interested in housework than in him, when she moved unhurriedly from the settee. Her cool front was like armour plating as she told him with a casual smile,

'I was just making a start on the ironing when you rang the bell, *monsieur*. Since you appear not to require refreshment of any sort, I'm sure you'll excuse me if I go and carry on with it.'

She did not miss the determined light in his eyes when he too left the settee. Overwhelmingly conscious of his height, and the forceful look of his chin, she had more things on her mind than the worry that he might think her manners as a hostess were near to being atrocious.

'I hope you don't think me rude,' she said carefully, as she made her way to the door, 'but we don't have any domestic help, and I don't like to leave the ironing until . . .'

'Brooke.' Jourdain spoke her name, and made her break off. Her hand was on the handle of the door but, somehow, she just could not turn it. Her throat felt choked, and she wanted to be away from him. But, as if his will was stronger than hers, he had only to speak her name for her limbs to become paralysed. Suddenly her casual air had deserted her.

'Yes?' she answered quietly, her voice strangely husky to her ears. Her adrenalin started to pump when she heard him move. Jourdain was close behind her when, his voice severe, he said,

'Since I saw you last, I have slept little and have worked fast, in order to return to my home where I

hought you were. I could not believe it when I found you
gone, but a telephone call to England told me that I
must.' She had nothing to say, but it was the hardest work
n the world to remain still as suddenly his hands came to
her upper arms and he went on, 'With you not where you
should be, there was nothing for it but to come straight
away to where you were. But, Brooke Farringdon,' he
said heavily, 'if you think I will go away—go out of your
life—without telling you what I have come to tell you;
without knowing for myself your true feelings, then
hérie, you must think again.'

His words made panic break afresh in Brooke. She had
no intention whatsoever of turning to face him, but when
his fingers tightened on her arms and he made her
stubborn feet move until she was indeed facing him, she
had to drag up every vestige of self-control which she
could find.

'Why did you come, *monsieur*?' she addressed the
jacket of the lightweight suit he had on, and the cool tone
she managed was a surprise to her when she considered
how she felt inside. She made herself go on, grabbing
back her control when it started to get away, 'What
exactly do you have to tell me?'

She was aware by then of his ability to see beneath her
outwardly composed façade, and would not allow him to
look into her eyes. As determined as he, she kept her
head bent. In the silence she heard him take a long-
drawn breath as if to steady himself, but it was she who
was fighting to stay steady, when he said quietly,

'*Je t'aime.*'

Brooke's head shot up. Her gaze incredulous, she
stared straight into his warm grey eyes. Her heart was
beating so rapidly then, her throat so suddenly dry, that it
took her several seconds before she could begin to

question his unbelievable statement.'

'You—it——' she started off badly. Then, 'Doe:
that—mean what I—think it means?'

'It means,' said Jourdain, his grip firm on her arms, hi
eyes drinking in every telltale nuance in her amazed
expression, 'that I love you, Brooke. That I love you with
all my heart, and with all my soul.'

Her mouth had started to form an 'O' of wonderment
She was not certain if she had not begun to beam a smile
of incredulous delight. Then, suddenly, she came
crashing to her senses. And it was the most terrible let
down of all. For a few short seconds she had let herself be
deluded into thinking that, as he said, Jourdain truly
loved her. But how could he?

As he saw her thunderstruck expression and the smile
that had so nearly made it, his eyes had the look of a man
who had started to believe that any coldness in her had
gone for ever. *His* incredulity was therefore unmistak
able when, in freezing tones, she requested bluntly,

'Would you mind very much, *monsieur*, taking your
hands off me.'

'Brooke!' he exclaimed. 'Have you not heard what
. . .?'

'I heard every word,' she told him waspishly. 'And I
believe none of it.'

'You think I would lie to you—and over such a . . .'

'What have you done all along but lie?' she exclaimed
angrily.

'When . . .'

'You wanted your revenge for the many times I
offended you. What better way than—when you knew I
couldn't wait to leave—to make me stay.'

'I've explained why I wanted you to stay,' he cut in
explosively. 'You intrigued me, I wanted to get to know

ou better. To . . .'

'You got to know me better all right!' Brooke flared.
Had it not been for . . .' her voice started to fade, but
nother upsurge of anger overcame her, and she went for
im again. 'The afternoon we called at the farm, you'd
ave made love to me—full love to me if . . .'

'I had already told you,' he sliced in, 'that I would not
arm you. *Mon Dieu*,' he growled. 'I wanted you that
fternoon as I have never wanted any woman. Was it the
ct of some man determined on—revenge—that I
ontrolled my urgent need for you?'

'Controlled!' she hurled at him, out of control herself,
nd for once uncaring of it. 'My memory is that you
ouldn't have cared less whether we made love or not!'

'You have so much experience of a man?' Jourdain
nterjected shortly. 'Believe me, it was torment to know I
ould have you if I persisted, yet to have to remind myself
f your virgin state, and hold back my desire. I feared
hat if I insisted we made love, I might frighten you away
nd could lose what chance I had with you for ever.'

'Chance!' she scorned.

Jourdain sent her an exasperated look. 'There was
nore on my mind than bed,' he told her bluntly, and
veathered her hostile look to tell her, his voice quieter
han it had been for some minutes, 'I want you in my bed,
f course I do, but not for some casual meaningless affair,
love you, I love everything about you. I knew I loved
ou on the day I listened to you speak with your father
ver the telephone. I knew when you held back from
elling him you believed that Stephanie had attempted
uicide what a lovely person you are. I knew, when I
eard you tell him you would soon be home, that I didn't
vant you to go. I knew then, that wherever you went, I
vanted to be there too.'

Her anger was suddenly gone, and she had the treacherous feeling she was going to wilt if Jourdain went on talking this way. 'I'll accept you wanted me in your home, even if I don't accept your version of the reasons,' she made herself reply and pressed on disagreeably, 'you must have been highly delighted, when, eating humble pie, I had to ask if I could stay on to look after my sister. It was, after all, what you planned.'

'It was,' he agreed solemnly. 'But I did not know then what was happening to me. I did not know that again and again I would suffer the compulsion to tell you there was nothing wrong with her, yet at the same time fear you might find out from someone else before I could tell you. I did not know of the murderous jealousy that would fill my heart when I heard you do such a natural thing as call Matthieu Delage by his first name when, stubbornly, you had refused to use mine. Nor did I know, my lovely Brooke,' he said softly, 'of the tenderness which would come over me when in the middle of the night I found you checking on Stephanie.'

Against the advice of her head, Brooke's heart stirred when she thought back to that night, and the words, 'You kissed my cheek,' fell from between her lips.

'You looked so vulnerable standing there with your beautiful blonde hair all fluffy about your head,' Jourdain remembered. 'It was not sex that reared its head when I saw you clad in only your nightdress, but a need to protect you. Such an urge came over me that it was all I could do not to gather you into my arms.

'But you didn't.'

'How could I, sweet love?' he asked, a smile in his voice. 'You would not have understood—as I did not fully understand myself then—why I wanted to enfold you in my arms and perhaps sleep with you in my bed ithout thought of sexual motives.'

What he had just said sounded so beautiful in her ears
at Brooke's heart gave another lurch. 'Was it for a
milar reason, for a reason you thought I might
isunderstand, that you didn't kiss me when we went out
dinner on Sunday evening?' she asked. Somehow her
ride that he might have seen her love for him that night
o longer seemed to matter. 'You said you wanted to,' she
minded him.

'I have forgotten none of what was the most
nchanting evening of my life.' Jourdain told her
nderly. 'The whole evening had been special for me,
nd, I hoped, for you too. I wanted quite desperately to
al what had been perfect for me with a kiss to your
outh—but two things stopped me in time.'

'What—two things?' she asked, a wild drumming in
er heart.

'One,' he replied, 'was that I was so weakened by that
nchanted evening, I could not be certain, as I was once
efore, that should you respond to my kiss I would be
ble to leave you to go up those stairs alone.'

Brooke remembered her feelings that evening, and
new she would have gone with him then, wherever he
d her and there was a breathless note in her voice when
he asked, 'The other—what was the other reason?'

'You were convinced I was a flirt, *ma mie*,' Jourdain
miled. 'It came to me, when I wanted to end our evening
ith an embrace, that you might misunderstand and
ink my motive that of a flirt expecting a return for the
vening.'

'Oh!' she exclaimed, her heart hammering, trust in
im taking her over, 'I never thought of that.'

'I had to think of it, *mignonne*,' he said gently. 'The two
ombined—my control already weakened, your idea of

me fixed firmly in your head—how could I kiss you?
knew I could delay leaving for Paris no later than v
early the next morning. Just as I knew that, should yo
awake in my bed and find me gone—no matter what w
had shared—I could cause you pain when you thought, a
surely you would, that I was nothing but a kiss-and-leav
philanderer.'

'Oh!' she breathed on a sigh. 'Oh, Jourdain,' she sai
huskily. When she could see he was waiting for her to sa
more, she suddenly realised what his deep and steadyin
breath had been all about. Because it took all of he
nerve, and a very deep breath, before she could tell hin
shakily, 'Ex-cuse my dreadful accent, but—*Je t'aime.*'

For long, long moments, that was all she did tell him
Because no sooner had the words shyly left her than sh
was in his arms. In the emotion of the moment, Jourdai
whispered in her ear softly breathed words of Frencl
which she could not understand. But when he pulle
back to look into her eyes there was nothing incompre
hensible about the utter joy she saw in his gaze.

'I think I shall have to learn French very quickly,' sh
murmured tremulously, and saw him realise only the
that he had spoken his words of joy and endearment ii
his own language. Then he kissed her, and with her han
against his heart, she could feel it thudding out the sam
wild beat as hers.

As if they had been starved of each other, one kiss wa
not enough. Minutes, joyous minutes ticked by. Some
how they had moved to the settee where Brooke thrille
to his caresses, and his words of love.

Jourdain was in charge, though, when passion stirred
Brooke had no will or wish to be anywhere but in hi
arms, but it was he who drew back, his hand leaving he
breast to cup the side of her face.

'Forgive me *ma mie*,' he whispered, his eyes adoring
er, 'I think knowing that you love me has made me
orget the courtesy I owe to your father's house.'

'You don't have to apologise,' Brooke told him huskily,
nd absolutely adored him when his smile appeared and
e teased,

'For such an innocent, *mignonne*, I fear there is a very
orward streak in you.'

Brooke laughed, in love with him, in love with life.
You don't think some of the blame may be yours, that
ew parts of my character, including that forward streak,
ave only shown themselves since I have known you?'

Jourdain grinned, then kissed her, but pulled back
efore that kiss could get out of hand. 'You too have been
stranger to yourself since love started to enter your
eart?'

Brooke nodded, 'I've always thought of myself as fairly
nflappable, and more or less capable of coping with
ost situations,' she told him, then confessed, 'I just
idn't recognise the person I was at your château. By
urns you made me laugh, get angry, and get so furious on
ccasions that I just went out of control. I'm sorry I hit
ou,' she apologised. She saw she was forgiven by his
mile, and his gentle kiss on her mouth.

'There were other emotions that were new to you too, I
hink,' he murmured, his gaze flickering to her mouth
nd back to her eyes.

'I'd never desired a man before, if that's what you're
sking, *monsieur*,' she said primly, but had to laugh at his
rowl at the word '*monsieur*'. It was at odds, though, with
is look of delight at the confession in her statement.
Nor,' she went on, her laughter fading, 'did I know, or
xpect to know, what jealousy felt like.'

'You were jealous! But of what—of whom?' Jourdain

enquired, mystified. 'I have not looked at anothe
woman, or wanted to, since I have known you. Surely yo
knew I had no interest in Stephanie, apart from my dut
to her?'

'Not Stephanie,' Brooke said quickly, and even thoug
she had started to feel a shade uncomfortable, now tha
she knew Jourdain loved her, she could hold nothin
back from him, 'Mélisande,' she told him.

'Mélisande!'

'Before I knew she was your niece,' she hurried t
clarify. 'I heard the sound of someone arriving in a hurry
and looked out of my bedroom window to see you an
Mélisande in each other's arms. It hurt dreadfully,' sh
said, and was promptly cradled in Jourdain's arms
where she went on, 'I just couldn't get the picture of th
two of you together out of my head. It was then,' sh
confessed, 'that I knew I was in love with you.'

More minutes of silence ticked by, when with gentl
tender kisses, Jourdain sought to banish the pain an
hurt she had known. He still had her cradled in his arms
when he told her of his jealousy over Matthieu Delage

'But I have never experienced such violent feeling,' h
went on, 'as the jealousy that raged in me when, out o
our walk that day, you told me you had some man waitin
for you in England.'

'So that's why you suddenly became so aggressive!' sh
exclaimed, startled, then had to smile as she remem
bered, 'you soon caught me out in that fib, though.'

Jourdain smiled too, and content, they sat with n
words needed, just enjoying the freedom they now ha
with each other.

'How glad I am, that I made that telephone call t
Mélisande,' Jourdain murmured into the contente
silence. 'Had she not come roaring up the drive an

stirred you to jealousy, you might still not have realised what it was that made you react so emotionally to me.'

'Oh, I think I would,' Brooke replied, the love she had for him so great that she was certain she would have discovered it not long afterwards. Then what he had just said hit her, and, startled again, 'You *sent* for Mélisande!' she exclaimed.

'Of course,' he replied. '*Naturellement*, I was in touch with her home every day to know how things were with her father. But when, to frustrate my schemes to be alone with you, you insisted on staying with Stephanie even to the extent of eating your meals with her—I had to draw up fresh plans. With Henri on the road to recovery, it was obvious to me that Mélisande would be better employed keeping Stephanie company. That way . . .'

'I would be free to—er—keep you company?'

'It worked, *n'est-ce pas?*' he grinned.

'It worked,' Brooke smiled happily. 'Even if you did have to kidnap me to take me out to dinner!'

'Ah, my Brooke,' Jourdain murmured, 'it was worth it. Even though,' he added with a rueful look, 'I became so enchanted with you that, by the time we were drinking our coffee, I almost chanced everything, and asked you to marry me, right then.'

Her sea-green eyes shot wide and for a moment she was incapable of speech. The memory then returned to her of how he had told her he must marry, and it was with a trace of anxiety that she questioned,

'But do you *want* to marry? I mean, you told me that night that there was no other way for you, because your children must have your name.'

'I told you there was no other way for me,' he confirmed gently. 'What I so nearly said, but did not, for fear I was going too fast and might ruin what looked to be a promising beginning, was that there is no other way for me but to marry you and none other.'

Brooke's throat was suddenly choked, but somehow she managed a shaky, 'You want to—marry me?'

'I love you, sweet Brooke, with all that is in me,' Jourdain said, his voice suddenly throaty at her shaken expression. 'You have been so busy looking after others, has it not occurred to you that someone might want to look after you? Will you, sweet love, let me be that someone? Will you join me in France?' he asked, the tension in him communicating itself to her. 'Will you, *mignonne*, do me the honour of becoming my wife?'

'Oh, Jourdain,' sighed Brooke on a whispered breath, his tension as he waited for her answer arousing the most tender of feelings inside her. 'I'd like very, very much, to become your wife.'

His tension broke, and in the next moment he had hauled her close up to him. Kisses rained down on her upturned face as well as words of endearment in French and in English.

There was no mistaking his joy when, at last he drew back and gazed into her eyes as if he could not have enough of looking at her.

'We will marry soon, Brooke?' he asked. 'Sometimes I can be very patient, but this is not one of those times. We can . . .' he began, when the sound of someone entering the house with hurricane force made him break off.

'Stephanie,' Brooke told him, but where once she would have called out to let her know which room she was in, this time she left it for her sister to come and find her.

Stephanie called 'Brooke!' They heard her go along to the kitchen and then come to the sitting-room door. It opened, and Stephanie did a sudden double-take at the two occupants of the settee, who looked for all the world as though something magical had happened for them.

'What . . . are you doing here?' she addressed Jourdain on a gasp as he got to his feet and, not wanting to be parted from Brooke drew her up with him.

'*Bonjour*, Stephanie,' said Jourdain politely, but in the face of Stephanie's look of amazement at seeing him there with his arm apparently glued around her sister, he could not keep up his pretence of formality. 'It's a long story,' he said, his smile quirking out. He sent a loving look to the girl he held close to his side. 'But if you are very good, I'm sure Brooke will allow you to be a bridesmaid at our wedding.'

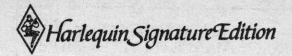

Carole Mortimer

Merlyn's Magic

She came to him from out of the storm and was drawn into his yearning arms—the tempestuous night held a magic all its own.

You've enjoyed Carole Mortimer's Harlequin Presents stories, and her previous bestseller, *Gypsy*.

Now, don't miss her latest, most exciting bestseller, *Merlyn's Magic*!

IN JULY

MERMG

Take 4 best-selling love stories FREE
Plus get a FREE surprise gift!